The Good,
The Bad,
and Ugly Creek

by

Cheryel Hutton

Ugly Creek Series, Book 5

This is a work of fiction. Names, characters, places, and incidents are either the product of the author's imagination or are used fictitiously, and any resemblance to actual persons living or dead, business establishments, events, or locales, is entirely coincidental.

The Good, The Bad, and Ugly Creek

Cover Art by *The Wild Rose Press, Inc.*

The Wild Rose Press, Inc.
PO Box 708
Adams Basin, NY 14410-0708
Visit us at www.thewildrosepress.com

Publishing History
First Edition, 2023
Print Trade Paperback ISBN 978-1-5092-4742-4
Digital ISBN 978-1-5092-4742-4

Ugly Creek Series, Book 5
Published in the United States of America

Logan moved to my side, brushed my hair back, and proceeded to examine my ear.

"What do you think you're doing?"

"Looking for a gullible bug."

Bug? Yikes! "You're looking for a what?"

"A gullible bug."

I stared at him, and he tipped his head to the side and looked right back.

"You're an intelligent woman who doesn't strike me as someone to fall for a trick like riding with a couple, so you'd be stuck helping them until they decided to take you back home. Therefore, you must have been slipped a gullible bug."

He made as if to pull something out of my ear, toss it on the floor, and stomped hard. "There you go. You're all safe from the ugly gullible bug for now, but don't let Devereux anywhere near your head. He's a devious one."

"You're nuts. You know that?"

Logan grinned. "Ah sugar, you say the sweetest things."

Also By Cheryel Hutton

The Ugly Creek Series
The Ugly Truth
Secrets of Ugly Creek
Doggone Ugly Creek
Tails of Ugly Creek

Keepers of Legend
Blood of the Innocent (Lobster Cove)

Dedication

This book is dedicated to my late husband, the hero in my own romance story, the love of my life. I will miss you every single day until we walk hand in hand through the next world. Rest well, my love.

Chapter 1

Tennessee really was beautiful, especially here at the foot of the Smoky Mountains. Tree-lined roads, some with small streams just a few feet away. A few places were cut stone from where the road wound through an area that was once part of the mountain. I rolled down my windows and enjoyed the fresh, cool feeling on my face. It was wonderful.

I was jolted from my happy contemplation by the sight of a particular tree. I was almost one hundred percent sure I'd already driven by that twisted, forked, and tired-looking thing before. Maybe twice. That's all I needed today, to go in circles. Like the drive from Florida to Tennessee wasn't long enough.

I glanced down at my cell to be sure it was still telling me I was on the right road, but a flash of color had me looking up again. A bright yellow convertible tore down the middle of the road and headed right at me! I aimed for the side of the road, only to realize a huge rock was in my way. Jerking the wheel at the last second, I missed the rock, then aimed for the side again. *Thump*!

The front passenger side dropped. Along with my heart. I took a moment to let my heart rate slow down enough it wouldn't burst out of my chest. The other driver didn't seem to be concerned at all that he could have killed me. He blew past and kept going. A glance at my phone showed me two bars, and told me I might just be able to get help way out wherever the hell I was.

The sound behind me kicked my heartrate back up, I looked back to see the rocket-car speed toward me. I held my breath until the car had stopped.

A man got out. Tall, black hair, nice body. Dressed in black jeans, black leather jacket, and dark sunglasses, he swaggered my way. I'd read the word many times, but I never really got it until now. This guy truly swaggered. I dialed nine-one-one on my cell and kept my finger on the button as I rolled down my window.

"Are you all right?" he asked.

"Other than being run off the road, stuck in a ditch, and still shaking, I'm excellent."

"Let's get your little shoe box car back on the road." He sauntered toward the front.

I opened the door, jumped out, and ran toward the front. "I have road service with my insurance. I'll call." I waved my cell phone.

"No need for that. I can shove this little thing out."

"The car could be damaged."

"I seriously doubt it, but we won't know until we get it out of the ditch." He straddled the ditch and put his hands against the car. "Back up slowly."

"But…"

He looked at me, and I could see exasperation on his face. "It'll just take a minute."

I gave up and went back to my car. "Fine."

"And please make sure you are backing up.

"I'll try."

I got in the driver's seat, slammed the door, and put my car in reverse. I pushed on the gas pedal, but nothing happened. I pushed a little harder. My tire rolled out of the hole and I was moving backwards.

Relief poured through me as I turned off the motor. I got out and went around to the front where the man was looking under the front of the car. "Is it okay?"

"Seems to be fine." He stood up, shoved those obnoxious dark sunglasses back on, and grinned. "You're welcome."

My jaw clenched. "You're the one who caused the problem in the first place. I wound up in the ditch to keep you from hitting me head-on."

"I wouldn't have hit you."

"Couldn't prove it by me."

He shrugged. "Nobody ever comes up this way so I wasn't expecting you. Of course, I'd have seen you sooner if you weren't driving a shoebox instead of a car. Let me guess, it's sensible."

"Sensible is not a bad thing."

"Nah, just boring." He grinned. "If you're okay, then I need to get going. I'm supposed to be on a beer run. Need anything?"

"No." I was amazed I could talk with my teeth and jaw clenched so hard.

The arrogant pain spun his yellow menace in an illegal U-turn, waved to me and headed toward his original direction. Maybe I should have asked him if I was actually headed toward Ugly Creek. Then again, I'm not sure I'd believe anything he said. I checked the map app and put the car in gear. If I didn't find the place soon, I'd call Terri to get directions.

As I started to pull out, movement caught my eye from the vicinity of a huge tree. I looked closer and saw what appeared to be the outline of a big, furry creature. My stomach flipped, and all my blood left the top of my body to hide in my legs.

It had to be a bear. Nothing else was that big and furry—unless, of course, you believed the Bigfoot stories that Ugly Creek is famous for. Seconds later, I remembered how small my car is and how big wild animals can get. Memories filled my mind of a movie T-Rex spinning a little car like a toy.

T-Rex, Bigfoot, or bear, it was time for me to leave.

I tore onto the road and headed as fast as was reasonably safe toward whatever was ahead. I didn't much care, as long as it wasn't hungry for people snacks.

To my surprise, just around the corner was a "Welcome to Ugly Creek" sign. Within minutes a few scattered houses changed to subdivisions. It wasn't long before my phone told me to turn onto a smaller road, then another. I saw the place before the emotionless phone voice could tell me, "Your destination is on the right."

The adorable house was white, with a matching picket fence. Nice big porch, with four square columns across the front. At the base of each, river rock bases widened the bottom into triangular bases. Wooden railings ran from the front to back and across, except for an opening at the entrance. The home was Craftsman style maybe, or bungalow. I wasn't sure, but I'd bet Terri knew.

Beautiful greenery and neatly trimmed hedges around the porch, some of which had berries and even flowers. Delicate light pink blossoms along with lavender Cyclamen. Not a place I'd have expected to find my unconventional best friend.

4

I pulled into the driveway, and before I could get out of the car, a familiar woman leaped off the porch and flew across the lawn toward me, her waist-length, honey-colored hair flying behind her. My heart warmed as my lips pulled into a huge, thankful smile. "Terri!"

"Dia!"

I met her halfway, and we wrapped our arms around each other.

"It's so good to see you!" Over her shoulder, I saw that a dark-haired man, as tall or taller than the idiot who'd run me off the road, stood on the porch, shifting from foot to foot and working at not looking our way. "Is that your new love interest?"

"Yes, that's Hunter." Terri's cheeks bloomed pink.

I didn't know whether to laugh, take a picture and put it on social media, or ask if she was all right. I'd never seen Terri Quinn blush, not in all the years I'd known her. The cause of her pink cheeks fought a grin. I took a couple of steps his way.

"Hello, Hunter. I'm Dia Grey."

He swung off the porch. "Hunter Deveraux. Nice to meet you, Dia."

I took his offered hand with a big dose of apprehension. I have an ability, and I never know what will happen when I touch somebody. But this nice man cared deeply for my friend.

"I won't be in your way, honest. I booked a room at Rosemary's Bed and Breakfast."

"Nobody called you?"

I didn't like the way his forehead creased or the sound of concern in his voice. I thought he might be setting me up for some kind of joke, but as I let go of his hand, I felt truthfulness.

Terri wrapped her arm around me. "I can't believe they didn't call you. The B&B had a fire a couple of days ago."

"Was anybody hurt?"

"Not seriously, and the building can be repaired. But Rosemary won't be able to take in guests until things are fixed."

"I'll find someplace else to stay."

"Rosemary's is the only place in Ugly Creek," Hunter said.

"That's why you're staying here." Terri had her stubborn face on, jaw set, shoulders back, standing very still, eyes narrowed and focused on me.

Stubborn or not, I didn't want to be a third wheel. "Oh no. I'm not intruding on you two. I'll just drive a little further out. Maybe Eagle Wing Lake, or something closer to Knoxville."

"It's not worth you driving when Shay stays at Ace's all the time," Terri said.

I smiled. "She does, does she?"

Terri's smile turned mischievous. "Yes, she does. Do you believe it?"

So the cousins, the two most non-social women I knew, were both seriously involved. "Tennessee's been good for the two of you."

Terri gave me a sideways hug as she leaned close. "Maybe it'll be good for you too."

"I hope so, but not in the way you're implying."

A vehicle pulled in behind me and I looked back. The color I saw was enough to have me groaning. That stupid rocket-car was sitting just behind mine.

"That didn't take long," Hunter said as he trotted toward the car.

The jerk driver handed Hunter a couple of six-packs, then reached back in for a grocery bag. "I went to that little store just outside of town."

"I always forget about that place," Hunter said. "Come and meet Terri's friend."

Jerk Driver followed behind him. "Well, hello, Ms. Sensible."

"You know each other?"

"Not really." He held out his hand. "I'm Logan Montgomery, a friend of Hunter's."

I opened my mouth, but Terri beat me to it. "Logan, this is Dia Grey, my best friend in the world."

"Nice to meet you, Dia Grey."

"Logan." I took his hand, expecting to get visions of all manner of wicked behavior along with a seriously self-centered attitude. What I actually got was…nothing. No visions at all, and only a faint whisper of interest, I wasn't even sure about who or what.

"Let's go inside and have dinner before the basketball game starts." Terri put an arm around my shoulders. "We'll get your stuff after we eat."

"I really don't want to invade your privacy."

"You won't. Besides, you just drove over six hundred miles. No way am I letting you back out there to drive some more."

"I am tired," I admitted.

"Trust me, girlfriend. I know how long that drive is."

We walked together into the modest white house. The place actually belonged to Terri's aunt, but it didn't look at all like a middle-aged woman's bland home.

I knew Terri and her mother were a

little…well…different. It appeared her aunt must be a little different too. In spite of the classic, unassuming exterior, the interior was bright and colorful. The furnishings were modern with a bohemian flair. From the bright blue couch and throw cushions of red, green, and sunshine yellow; to the pottery pieces that looked Native American, to the huge purple dream-catcher hanging behind the mismatched armchairs it was awesome. I felt right at home.

We went through the living room into the eat-in kitchen. On the table, bread, meat, cheese, and every other fixin' I could imagine were lined up. Along the sides, disposable cups and plates were covering the counter. Hunter opened the fridge, and colas, iced tea, and beer were cooling and ready. The men wasted no time grabbing plates. While they tried to see how much food they could balance on a paper plate, Terri showed me the rest of the house.

"The master suite, which is the one Aunt Ruth uses, is over here back behind the formal dining room," Terri told me. "We leave her personal area alone. The only time we've been in there was after the tornado to make sure everything was okay."

My heart skipped a beat, recovered, and skipped another. "Tornado? You didn't tell me you had a tornado. Why didn't you mention that?"

Terri grinned and patted my shoulder. "They're rare here, I promise. It wasn't even that big. It was just really scary."

"Scary? You said this place is quiet, and nothing ever happens here."

My best friend shrugged. "Mostly nothing does."

"Mostly, huh? Like not every day?"

She laughed, the rat. "Like not every year. This place is mostly boring."

"If it is really that boring, why do you like it here?"

"Because Hunter isn't boring."

I rolled my eyes, but deep down, a tiny quiver of envy prodded me. It seemed every woman I knew was seeing somebody. Then again, I certainly wouldn't want to be in my sister's shoes.

"Both Shay and I found our soulmates here," Terri said. "Maybe you'll find yours here too."

I sighed. "Why would I want a man? They're more trouble than they're worth."

"That's what I used to say." Terri waved her hand in game show model fashion. "This is Shay's room. You can sleep in here."

The room was clean and uncluttered. There was a chest and nightstand and a small desk, all light wood. The bed was topped with a purple and green cover. On the bed were a rope and a package of chocolate chip cookies. I picked them up and looked at my friend.

"I told you that if you came here, I'd have those for you."

"I didn't think you meant literally."

She shrugged. "You never know when you might need them."

"You're sure Shay won't have a problem with me staying here?"

"I told you, she stays with Ace most of the time."

"What if she and Ace argue, or she just wants some time away from him?"

Terri leaned closer. "Then we'll throw Hunter out, and you can share my room."

"You're nuts," I told her.

"Thank you."

We laughed as we walked back into the kitchen. The men had already taken out a noticeable portion of the food, and were talking in the living room. We filled our own plates and joined them. Terri sat next to Hunter on the overstuffed blue couch and curled her feet under her. Logan was in the matching chair, so I took the only other seat, an extremely comfortable chair, it turned out. I hadn't realized how hungry I was, and the sandwiches tasted awesome.

The conversation was mostly between the other three. Terri or Hunter would occasionally try to pull me in, but I was too tired to talk much. At halftime, Terri and I went out to my car to get necessities for the night, then sat back down to watch the rest of the game.

I like basketball okay, but I'm not a huge fan. My stomach was full. I was relaxed for the first time since the break with my sister, and it had been a very long drive. My thoughts swam to my smart, beautiful sister. I know her fiancé is cheating on her, but she refuses to believe me. Now she refuses to speak to me.

I kept dozing off, but Hunter's and Logan's excited yells woke me when anything happened. It was an interesting game, but I knew I should excuse myself and go to bed. It would be rude, but so would snoring. In a few minutes, I promised myself.

Just a few more minutes.

****

Someone big and strong was carrying me. Um, what a nice dream. I enjoyed the feeling of being in a man's arms.

"Okay, the bed's turned down."

Terri's voice. Wait, what? Dang, if this was real, I

owed my hosts big time. But I'd think about that later.

"Here you go, Ms. Sensible. Sleep tight."

There were footsteps, and the door closed. My eyes popped open, and I lay in shock, wondering if I'd imagined Logan's voice.

Fortunately, I was too tired to think about it for very long.

Chapter 2

I woke to the enticing smell of coffee and the feel of a warm, soft ball of fur curled next to me. "Well, hello, Scrappy." I smiled at the adorable white and amber cat. I carefully moved her and threw back the covers. And discovered I was fully dressed except for my shoes.

The previous night charged back at me. Forever long drive, Yellow Menace, food, basketball, exhaustion, being carried to bed. I would like to believe that last part was a dream or hallucination. Man, what kind of a pathetic house guest was I?

I grabbed clean clothes and personal items, then slipped out into the hall to where I hoped I remembered the bathroom. After a quick shower and morning routine, I was more willing to face up to whatever happened.

In the kitchen, I stopped and drew in a long, full breath of the wonderful aroma. "Coffee!"

"There's plenty if you want some. Mugs in the cabinet above the coffee maker, sugar on the counter, and milk in the fridge."

I grinned at Hunter, who sat at the kitchen table with a laptop in front of him. I poured some coffee and a splash of milk into my cup and took a long sip. "Yum. I take it you're the one who made this. I can't tell you how nice it was to wake up and smell coffee."

Hunter chuckled. "I gotta say, it feels good to have another coffee drinker in the house."

"So you haven't been able to convert Terri?"

"No, she's still a dedicated tea drinker."The doggie door built into the kitchen door flipped open, and a collie burst through. The dog, whose name was Trixie, executed some sort of odd twisty stretch, swirled a moment, then became Terri.

I quickly averted my gaze. It was interesting, and pretty amazing to witness a were-dog change into a woman. It was less interesting to watch as my naked best friend kissed her man. I caught a glimpse of Hunter's reddened face and decided I wasn't the only one uncomfortable with my best friend's lack of modesty.

"Still get embarrassed easily, huh?" Terri looked straight at me.

"I just don't like seeing a naked collie. Trixie needs a collar."

She rolled her eyes. "How about we go explore Ugly Creek?"

"I'd like that."

Terri had talked so much about the quirky little town; I couldn't wait to see it for myself.

She leaned over the back of Hunter's chair and slid her hands down his chest. "Wanna go with us, handsome?"

He smiled at her, his expression so filled with love I had to blink back a tear. Would a man ever look at me with anything approaching that level of caring? I hoped so.

"I need to work, sweetheart," Hunter said. "I didn't get two thousand words written before daylight, like somebody we know."

"Almost three thousand today," she said.

He groaned. "It figures."

"I'd be happy to wake you up in the morning so you can be done before lunch."

"That's okay. As far as most people are concerned, three a.m. is the middle of the night."

"Humans are so pathetic."

I gazed out the window. The coffee cup hid my smile.

She pulled on the clothes she'd left in the kitchen, and grabbed her keys. "Ready to go?"

"Sure, just let me get my jacket and purse."

"You could feed your guest before you drag her out, you know."

She shot a frown Hunter's way, then back to me. "You haven't eaten yet?"

"No, but I'm not a big breakfast girl."

Terri sighed. "I remember that. I don't know how you survive for hours on coffee."

"The same way you survive without sleep," I told her.

"But I take naps to make up for it."

"I know," I said. "Lots of naps." I considered the idea for a moment. "You know, you probably get more sleep than the rest of us."

There was a quiet chuckle from Hunter's direction, and she narrowed her eyes. "Let's go." She headed off toward the living room.

I grabbed my purse and jacket and hurried after her. She was halfway to her car before I caught up, I slid in, and we headed off into the maze of Ugly Creek Roads.

She flipped on her signal light, and turned down a road that took us closer to the forest than where Terri lived. Less than five minutes later, she pulled into the driveway of an adorable little house. Or at least it would be adorable if it was an actual color and not faded gray, the porch didn't slope sideways, and if most of the windows weren't covered with wood scraps. The place had obviously been abandoned for quite some time.

"What do you think?"

I wondered what she was talking about, then saw the "for sale" sign with "pending" on top. "You're buying it."

"Hunter and I are." She grinned. "What do you think?"

I looked at the house. Bricks were pulling loose in several places on the foundation; some of the windows were broken, and the roof looked kinda sketchy. Still, it had a certain charm. The structure formed an L-shape. There was a bay window (more wood than window) on the right side, and the porch wrapped around the rest of the long front and down the side. The windows were small, but there were a lot of them.

"It's cute."

"It's better close up." Terri slid out of the car and headed toward the house. Of course I followed her. How could I not be curious what sort of house Terri would choose to purchase?

She didn't have a key, so we peeked in the windows. She was right; the inside was much nicer. Yes, there was some junk, drapes that had fallen from a window, a mattress, scattered wadded papers, and even a poor neglected doll, left by the previous owners. The place obviously needed a good cleaning, but it wasn't wrecked or anything.

"I'm not into 1950s' bathrooms. And that color's gotta go."

I went to stand beside her. The bathroom was definitely old-fashioned. Pink tiles with black accent. "So, you don't like retro?"

"Not in pink. It has a good layout, though." Her whole body vibrated, reminding me of the dog within her.

We walked around, checking windows as we went. Large rooms, plenty of space. "This place is nice."

"It has potential."

The kitchen had me giggling. "You definitely should keep that wallpaper."

A low growl sent chills up my spine. I'd known my friend most of my life, but I still glanced over my shoulder to make sure there wasn't a huge animal back there.

"How the heck do you make that sound with a human throat?"

"Talent. And I thought I'd save the wallpaper and kitchen cabinets for when you buy a house."

"I'm stuck in the seventies, huh?"

She gave me a big-eyed, innocent expression as she shrugged. "What can I say? When I saw the kitchen, I thought of you."

I rolled my eyes and shook my head. "You're so sweet."

"I know." Her smile faded. "What do you think, really?"

"I think it has serious potential."

"I'm still afraid something's going to go wrong.

We've been waiting almost two months for the closing."

"So you're really going to stay in Ugly Creek?"

She smiled. "I love this crazy town."

"And Hunter?"

"Him too."

"I'm happy for you."

"Thank you."

She grabbed me in a hug that came close to squeezing all the air out of my lungs. She finally let go, and we headed back to her car.

She drove, as usual, with the windows down, long hair flying, her chin up, a contented smile on her face. She kept stretching toward her door, so the wind hit her more.

"Would you like me to drive, so you can put your head out the window?"

"Not today, thank you." Her voice was serious.

I smiled to myself as I leaned back to watch the neighborhood go by. "This is a beautiful area."

"It ain't ugly."

I snorted. She stuck her tongue out at me, and I laughed in spite of myself.

I got a narrow-eyed glare, though Terri's lips were twitching. She tried to hold the expression, but a few seconds later, we were both laughing. It was so great to be with my friend again. I hadn't realized how much I missed her.

When we reached the outskirts of the town, we drove around, while my friend and tour guide pointed out the historical courthouse and some of the highlights of Ugly Creek's downtown. For instance, there was Out of the Blue Flea Market, Retreat thrift store, and the Arcane Restaurant and Magical Supply Shop. When she pulled into a parking space in front of Jake's Antiques, I figured this was her favorite store because of the variety of scents. With Terri being half-dog, she loves to smell things, especially older things, because they carry more history, more variety, more information.

Then we entered the store, and I reconsidered. The place was clean and beautifully arranged. I would have been happy to spend hours just looking at the wide variety. Then I caught a glimpse of Terri's nose twitching and smiled to myself. There might be plenty of other reasons, but she still enjoyed the rich scents.

"Hello, Terri. How are things?"

"Fine. How are you, Stephie? Feeling better?"

Stephie was a small woman, just a hair taller than my five-one. She was adorable, especially with the little bulge of her belly. My curiosity was killing me, but I wasn't about to ask in case I was wrong. Maybe I would shake her hand when we were introduced.

"I'm much better now that the morning sickness has stopped."

Well, that answered my question.

"Stephie, this is Dia, my best friend in the whole world."

"Dia! It's so nice to meet you finally." Stephie held out her hand, and I took it with a mix of curiosity and concern.

"Nice to meet you too."

Her happiness washed over me. This woman was content in her life, crazy in love with her husband, and thrilled about the tiny life growing inside her.

"Do you know the gender yet?"

"Not yet. I'm pulling for a girl, but Jake wants a boy. Honestly, though, we'd be happy with either."

I didn't tell her she would get exactly what she wanted. Instead, I asked her about a set of antique china similar to a set my grandmother had when I was a kid.

We chatted as we looked at more of the awesome antiques in Stephie's shop. I had a great time, but more customers trickled in until we decided to go away and let Stephie take care of her store. So we said a quick goodbye and headed down the street.

There were no big box stores here, no chain names everybody knows. Only a small town feel. These streets were filled with modest businesses run by everyday folks. It was a town caught in the fabric of time past. I could literally feel the rich history of the place that permeated the rocks, trees, and buildings. The feeling was similar to the wind, a stirring around me. Out of the corner of my eye, I caught a glimpse of a woman in 1920s' clothing. I smelled burning wood, and heard the sounds of horses coming down the street. The sound of multiple conversations pulled my attention from one place to another. It was confusing and odd, but it was also incredible.

"Are you still with me?"

I shook myself out of the reverie and turned to Terri.

"You were lost in your own world." She shrugged. "Which I totally understand. I just wanted to make sure you were okay. Ugly Creek can have peculiar effects on people."

I smiled. "I can feel the history, actually feel how this place was a hundred or more years ago."

She stood there, barely moving. "Wow. I had no idea you could do that."

"I can't. At least I never could before. You told me

there was something different about this town, but I never imagined anything like what I've experienced walking down this street."

"Is it a good feeling?"

"That's a hard question to answer. It just kind of is. Like life, there's good and bad all mixed up in a kaleidoscope of people, things, and events." I smiled. "Being able to feel it, that's incredible."

"That's seriously amazing."

"It is." My heart jumped a little, reminding me of how grateful I was for Terri's friendship. "Thanks for letting me hang with you. I hate being a third wheel."

"Don't worry; the B&B will open back up soon." She seemed to think for a moment. "Or I could send you to Abu Dhabi."

"You're a dog. You can't be a big orange cat."

"You aren't a cat or a dog, so I can send you anywhere I want."

We laughed as we headed down the sidewalk. We'd started to cross over to Mockingbird Lane when I saw a familiar yellow car parked in front of a brick building. Several other vehicles were parked nearby, but there were no signs or other indication of what went on in the building.

"That's where Logan works," Terri said.

The comment caught me by surprise. "I thought you said there weren't any corporations within the city limits of Ugly Creek."

She yawned, and I wondered if her early morning writing schedule might have to give in a little for other interests. Like that handsome man of hers, for example.

"There aren't any. Only small family businesses or small partnerships."

"But doesn't he work for a large corporation?"

"Yes, he does. This is a temporary facility where New Century Research and Development is coordinating their latest project."

"What kind of project?"

"That's mostly a secret, but what the company told the community leaders is that they plan to test indigenous plants for possible uses. Their hope, so they say, is to find cures for diseases or ways to help save the planet."

Maybe I'm just especially cynical, but that didn't seem like the goals of any big company I'd ever heard of. I tilted my head and squinted to see if I could get some kind of read on the place. Then I caught a glimpse of my friend's face. "Sounds wonky to you too, huh?" I asked.

Terri grinned. "I was hoping you'd agree with me. I didn't want to say anything to Hunter based just on my feelings, but if you got some kind of vibe from Logan, then there must be something."

I bit my lower lip as I studied the plain rectangular structure. "I, um, I didn't get a vibe from Logan."

"Really? So, what makes you think there's something wrong with this picture?"

"Same as you, logic along with gut feeling."

She wiggled a minute before she said, "So, what did you get from Logan?"

"Nothing."

"Don't do that to me, Dia. Come on, give me something."

I sighed. "I'm telling you the truth. You know me, I almost always get a visual from every person I touch, but not from Logan. In fact, this is the first time in my life I didn't at least get at least a strong feeling from a person I touched."

She blinked and stared at me. "Is he completely human?"

It was my turn to blink and stare. "Why? Do you think he might not be?"

"Not really. I was just wondering if he was something you can't read." She shrugged. "What other reason could there be for you not reading anything from him?"

I groaned. "I have no idea, Terri. I'm the only person I know who can do what I do. I don't know what it means that I can't read Logan. For all I know, there's just nothing in his brain to read."

Terri chuckled. "You really don't like Logan, do you?"

"He almost ran me over the night I arrived."

Her eyes widened, but her expression was more curiosity than empathy. "You're kidding."

My right eye twitched. "Nope. His yellow rocket-mobile came flying around a curve, and I had to aim for the ditch. Almost scared my stomach out of me. I had to sit there for a few minutes and put my nerves back inside my skin."

"Yeah, he does get a little carried away with that car of his. Hunter teases him that he had to get a bright color so that people know he's coming."

"It wasn't like that. He was going too fast. I could have been hurt, and he didn't seem to care." Tears filled my eyes, and I turned away to keep her from seeing.

"Are you okay?"

"I can't believe you're acting like it was nothing. You're my friend. I expected you to take me seriously.

Somebody's going to get hurt if he keeps on driving like that."

"Dia." She put a hand on my shoulder. "I'm sorry. I didn't mean to make it sound like I'm not concerned about you, or was dismissing what happened. I'll talk to Logan, or ask Hunter to, or both. He acts like a spoiled kid sometimes, and he needs to grow up."

I nodded as I wiped my face. I still couldn't face her. "I'm sorry, it wasn't my intention to fall apart on the street."

She gave me a sideways hug. "Don't worry about it. I should have been more understanding. You're here because your family won't listen, then I proceed not to listen."

"Terri…"

She shook her head. "Don't even. Let's go to the Bean Cup and get you coffee and me tea, and we'll talk."

"Sounds good." We started toward the other direction, and we hadn't gone more than a few steps before I remembered something Terri had said. "Since when does Ugly Creek have a coffee shop?"

"About a month ago. Apparently, they put it in just for you."

I grinned and tossed my head like I was a movie star. "That was very nice of them. I guess I should give out autographs."

"You just do that."

We giggled as we strolled into the shop, not meeting each other's gaze so we could hold it together long enough to get our drinks. By the time we sat at a corner table, we'd calmed down.

"Sorry about disparaging Logan."

"He's not my friend," she said. "I barely know the guy."

"But he and Hunter are buddies."

She tilted her head to the side for a moment. "They knew each other in college. I don't think they've seen much of each other since then."

I considered that. "They went to the same college? Not what I'd have thought."

"Why not?"

"Hunter is a serious, very intelligent man, and you told me he's a professor. Doesn't seem like the kind of school Logan would go to, or, to be honest, the kind of guy he'd hang with."

A smile pulled at Terri's face. "Don't judge a man by his attitude, girl. Logan has a master's in biology and a doctorate in biochemistry. He's worked in biotechnology since he was in graduate school."

"You're kidding!"

"Nope. Hunter and Logan are a good match as far as education is concerned."

"But not personality, right?" I was losing faith in my ability to size people up. Still, I knew what I saw with my own eyes.

She shrugged. "Hunter's eccentric, but he's cautious. I told you how long it took for him to believe I was a were-dog."

"Logan seems kind of reckless."

"Yeah, I'd thought so, but his almost running into you was definitely negligent."

"Look, I don't want to cause issues between you and Hunter."

"You won't. Hunter already knows something about Logan rubs me the wrong way. He listens, but I wouldn't ask him to give up his friendship because of my feelings about Logan. Especially since I don't really know him that well."

I sighed. "Relationships are hard."

"Nah, you just have to learn how to give and take."

"How's that going?" I bit back the smile.

"Lots of trial and error."

"Hello, Terri," someone said.

She sprang of her seat like she'd been poked and hugged the tiny white-haired woman. "Aunt Octavia! It's wonderful to see you."

"It's always good to see you too." The woman patted Terri on the cheek, then turned to scrutinize me. "Who's your gifted friend?"

"This is Dia. We grew up together down in Jacksonville. We've been best friends most of our lives."

I'd heard about this "Aunt Octavia" person, but I had no real idea what to expect from her. I stood to greet her and discovered she was even shorter than I am. She was dressed in bright pink sweatpants, jacket, and even matching sneakers. She had short, curly white hair, a cute little nose, and wide blue eyes. She was the most adorable little old lady I'd ever seen.

She reached for my hand, turned it over, and rubbed her fingertips over my palm. "You have an exceptionally strong gift."

Chills zig-zagged through me, and I looked past her toward the huge window at the front. "No, not me. You must be mistaken."

Aunt Octavia took my chin in her fingers and moved my face so that we were eye-to-eye. "The first step is to accept who you are and what you are capable of accomplishing."

"The first step to what?"

She smiled. "To finding your unique path." She dropped her hand and turned back to Terri. "Help your friend to find her path just as you found yours. Support her and guide her."

Aunt Octavia turned and strode out like she was a much younger woman. We looked at each other.

"Wow," I said.

"*I'm* supposed to *guide* you?" Terri's voice was almost an octave higher than usual. "Has the woman ever heard of the blind leading the blind?"

I smiled at my wide-eyed friend. "Hey, at least the people around you believe you can really do what you do."

She grinned. "It's hard to ignore a big old furry dog."

"True."

We laughed the tension away, then took our drinks with us as we walked around the awesome little town for another couple of hours. Eventually we headed back to Terri's house. Hunter had left a note that he was going to the library to do some research, Terri took a nap, and I tried reading a new thriller I'd been dying to get into.

I couldn't focus, though. I just kept thinking about Aunt Octavia. She had somehow known about my gift, and incredibly she'd nailed me for exactly what I was and what I did. I'd heard about Aunt Octavia from Terri for years, and I knew she was supposed to be an amazing psychic and a pretty awesome person. I couldn't help but wonder what she could teach me.

And if I had the courage to ask her if she would.

Chapter 3

Back at Terri's aunt's house, Hunter and Logan perched on the porch steps. They each held a bottle of beer and seemed to be having a great time. Terri climbed out of her car, and I followed suit.

"We'll get your things into the house later today," she said.

"I'd appreciate your help."

A few steps back from the porch, Hunter met Terri with a kiss. "Did you ladies enjoy yourselves?

"Why yes, we did," Terri spoke in a thick Southern accent. "We sat on the veranda and sipped lemonade while we spoke harshly of the damn Yankees."

"My sweet honeysuckle." He had a decent handle on his own Southern accent. "You don't need to worry your pretty little head about the invaders from the cold, harsh North. We big, strong Southern men will take care of that dirty business."

She lay her palm against his cheek. "Ah, but you men couldn't take care of the 'dirty business' without your women's help."

He executed a formal bow. "It is true. Our beautiful women are the brains. We are but the brawn."

Logan eyed the couple. "Laying it on thick there, aren't you, Devereux?"

Hunter grinned. "It's called thoroughly enjoying myself."

"Seems silly to me."

Hunter clasped Terri's face between his hands and studied her features with a deep expression of love. "Maybe one day you'll find out how much fun verbal sparring can be. If you ever find a woman who'll put up with you."

"Whatever."

Hunter shrugged, then pulled Terri against him and dove deep into a kiss. Her legs trembled and her fingers grabbed at his shirt. Wow. I gotta admit, I'd give a lot to experience that kind of love. Maybe someday I would. I swallowed the ache and looked away from the couple.

"Showoff," Logan muttered.

Hmm, I think I might not be the only one with a tiny bit of jealousy. I glanced his way, only to find myself caught in his gaze. I tried to untangle our connection, but even through the dark lenses of his sunglasses, his intensity held me.

Finally, the kissing couple pulled apart, and Hunter announced he was going after another drink. "Anybody want anything?"

"Another beer would be appreciated," Logan said.

Hunter looked at me. "Dia?"

"I'd like a cola, please."

"Coming right up." He turned to Terri. "Come with me. I have something to tell you."

They went into the house, and I was left alone with Logan.

"I knew something was up," Logan said. "Hunter's been antsy ever since I got here."

"I hope it's something good."

"Oh, I'm pretty sure it is."

He smiled at me, and I caught caring in his

expression. Well, that surprised me. He might not be the nicest person, but the man cared about his friends.

Squeals and then laughter were loud enough to startle me. A couple of minutes later, Hunter and Terri came back out onto the porch.

"We're closing on the house tomorrow!" Terri hugged me, then Logan, then Hunter—who got a hug *and* a kiss.

A long, involved kiss.

"That's awesome news," I said.

"Yeah," Logan muttered as he pointedly turned away from the couple.

They looked at us as if they'd forgotten we were even there.

"We're going out to celebrate." Hunter said. "You two want to go?"

They deserved to celebrate alone.

"No, thanks. Logan and I will be fine here."

Logan looked my way, but I couldn't see his eyes through his sunglasses. Still, I was fairly certain he was wondering where I got off making a decision for him. I ignored him and smiled at the happy couple.

"We'll be back soon," Terri said, and they headed toward Hunter's car.

"So, you couldn't wait to be alone with me, huh?"

"Keep dreaming, bud."

He slid off his sunglasses and narrowed his eyes at me. "You're nothing like I thought you'd be."

Well, that took me off guard. "You thought about me?"

He nodded. "Terri talked about you quite a bit. She said you're better than hotdogs for breakfast."

I laughed, "No way."

He held up one hand. "She really said it. Honest."

"High praise coming from her."

He grinned. "So, you've known her a long time."

"Since kindergarten."

"Awesome."

"Well, we were both outsiders, so we kinda hung together."

He wiggled a little as if fleas were biting him, but he was trying to ignore it. "They never got our drinks."

"I'm not surprised. They were wound up over their house. I'll go get them."

"I'll go." Logan started toward the door but stopped and looked over his shoulder. "That house sounds like a lot of work to me."

I started to say it would be worth a little hard work but his deep brown eyes, full lips, and amazing body distracted me. He was seriously handsome without sunglasses and with a smile on his face. Before I could gather my thoughts, he disappeared into the house. It only took him a couple of minutes to get the drinks and reappear. Clearly, he was familiar with Terri's kitchen. Then again, a fridge is hard to miss.

He handed me a cola, and as he sat down, I realized he was opening one himself. "I thought you wanted a beer." I shrugged and tried to look nonchalant. "Not that it's any of my business."

"I enjoy drinking with Hunter, but not while keeping company with a pretty lady."

My face warmed, and I looked down like a shy sixteen-year-old. I didn't even like him, and he had me blushing. I wanted to say something interesting, but before I thought of anything, my phone played the opening notes of "Superstition." I pulled it out, saw who the caller was, set the thing on vibrate, and stuck it back in my bag.

"Didn't want to talk?"

"It was my mother, no doubt calling to tell me what an ungrateful daughter I am."

"Oh."

He stared out toward the forest, elbows on his knees, shoulders hunched forward, and his chin down. He seemed sad, but a quick touch of his shoulder gave me nothing.

"Did I say something wrong?"

He shook his head without looking at me. "None of my business."

It was obvious something wasn't right, but what should I do? It was never like this for me. I could always tell what the other person was feeling. Then I'd go from there. But I was getting nothing from the man beside me.

I twisted a bit like I was stretching my back and touched him briefly on the bare skin of his arm. Nothing. I returned my hand to my lap and worked at shoving my own emotions back inside me. "What did I do wrong?"

He looked me in the eye. "I just think you maybe should be able to take five minutes from your busy vacation to speak to your mother."

I shook my head, hoping it would clear my thoughts. It didn't. "What is it with you? First, you try to run me over, and now you have the audacity to imply that you know more about my relationship with my mother than I do."

He stared at me, frowning hard as he did. "Say what? I didn't try to run over you."

I straightened my back and gave a tiny shrug. "Maybe it wasn't deliberate, but you weren't watching what you were doing. You can't come flying down the middle of the road and not expect that somebody might get hurt."

"Well, if you drove a real car and not a shoebox on wheels, maybe I'd have seen you."

"Seeing me isn't the issue. Speeding and taking up the whole road, that's the issue."

"I wasn't taking up the whole road, and I wasn't going that fast."

"Fast enough." I was so mad I shook, and he was completely ignoring my point. So I shifted the conversation. "And you have no right to comment on my relationship with my mother."

He locked gazes with me, and I swear electricity zinged between us.

"No, I don't, but if I could talk to my mom again for five minutes, I'd be the happiest man in the world."

He stalked out to his car, where he stood leaning against the ugly yellow thing and staring off into space. I walked as nonchalantly as I could up the steps to the porch and into the house. I went into my borrowed bedroom and closed the door, barely making it before sudden tears filled my eyes and flowed down my cheeks.

What the heck was I crying about? I was not about to let some spoiled rich kid get to me. I was just tired, that's all. By tomorrow I'd be fine. I wiped my face then sat on the bed and paged through some celebrity magazine. There was nothing in there that looked at all interesting.

Eventually I realized I was getting hungry. I forced

myself to wait until I thought I could confront Logan again without bursting into tears, then grabbed a bologna sandwich and sat out on the back steps. I didn't check out front, but Logan wasn't in the house. Either he was gone, or he didn't want to see me any more than I wanted to see him.

It was a couple of hours still before Terri and Hunter returned.

"Dia, are you here?" she yelled from inside.

"On the back steps," I yelled back.

Terri came out and sat beside me. "Sorry we deserted you."

"Don't worry about it. I'm happy for you two. Besides, I needed time to think."

"I take it you and Logan didn't enjoy each other's company."

"Oil and water. No biggie. Tell me about this house. How much serious renovation do you think it will take to make it the way you want it?"

She shot me a look that let me know she knew there was more between Logan and me, but went with the change in subject. For now.

"I know the house looks rough, but it's an amazing place. It's an Arts and Crafts bungalow built in 1908, It's been renovated a couple of times, and the basic structure is still solid."

Her words came out of her mouth so fast they tripped over each other, and she toyed with the hem of her t-shirt. "In an old house like that, we're likely to run into electrical or plumbing issues, hopefully not both. It passed inspection, and we didn't see anything obvious, but we'll need to pull everything out of the kitchen and bathroom. We want to put in a second bathroom too, but we plan on fixing the basics first." She grinned. "I can't believe we're finally closing. I was beginning to believe it was never going to happen."

My heart lifted, and took my spirits with it. It was great seeing my friend so excited. "What color are you going to paint the exterior?"

She tipped her head to the side and stilled for a moment. "We haven't even thought about what color we want."

"You have time. It sounds like you two have a lot of work to do."

"Yeah, but it'll be worth it."

I gave her an impulsive hug. "If you need an extra pair of hands, let me know."

The laugh sounded just a little bit evil. "I will."

She smiled and headed back into the house, leaving me wondering what I'd gotten myself into.

****

I sprawled on the bed and stared at the ceiling for a while. When darkness fell, and my mind was still swirling through memories of the day, I decided to go out on the back porch, sit on the steps, and contemplate where my life was going.

My sheltered friend was breaking out into the world. A man who I couldn't read but I was somehow attracted to was driving me nuts. And a woman who was widely admired said I have a strong gift, which, after having my ability denied for so many years, was mind-boggling.

I had to talk to Aunt Octavia again. If I could convince her to be my mentor, I'd be the happiest psychic around. But what chance did I have for that?

I made a mental note to ask Terri how to contact

Aunt Octavia. The woman had to have an address or phone or email or smoke signal or something. She was my best chance at getting a handle on my *gift* or *talent* or *curse* or whatever the hell it was. Which would be good because right now, my "gift" had a hold on me.

****

The next morning I sat at the kitchen table, chatting with Hunter while Terri continued her early morning writing session. Apparently, her muse just wouldn't let her go.

"Are you looking forward to renovating your house?" I asked him.

"Honestly, I'm excited, but I'm also intimidated." He twisted his coffee mug one way and then back. "It's something we've both wanted to do for a while, but neither of us have experience with renovation or construction. We can hire contractors, of course, but that would not only be expensive, it would kind of defeat the purpose of trying to do what we can by ourselves."

"I don't have experience either, but I'd be happy to help out where I can."

Hunter grinned. "You might regret that sometime in the future, but until you do, thanks."

"It should be interesting at the very least."

He looked down at his coffee for a moment, then back at me. "By the way, Logan has offered to help us out too."

I swallowed my apprehension. "Thanks for the heads-up."

"Dia, I know he can be a pain at times, but he's not a bad guy, honest."

"He's spoiled; that's what he is."

Before Hunter could refute my opinion, my cell rang. One look at the damn thing, and I groaned.

"Excuse me," I said as I headed out the back door to the porch. "Hello, Mom."

"Diara Casen Grey, what do you think you're doing?"

I rolled my eyes. My whole name. Great. So Mom was wound up more than usual. "I'm visiting my closest friend. You remember Terri, don't you?"

"And visiting this friend is more important to you than helping your sister prepare for her wedding?"

"It's more complicated than that."

"Yes, she told me about your *vision* and how you're using that as an excuse to ruin the most important day of her life."

I silently counted to ten in every language I knew how and made another couple up. When I thought I could speak without screaming, I attempted to make my point. "Number one, this is between Finley and me. Number two, after all these years, how can you dismiss my gift like that?"

"Gift?" Mom's voice climbed an octave. "So you're calling that little parlor trick of yours a gift now, are you?"

"It isn't a trick, and you know it."

"I know nothing of the kind. All I know is that Finley is very upset."

My stomach churned. I closed my eyes and leaned my forehead against the porch support post. "I don't want Finley to be hurt."

"Then stop this nonsense and come home!"

"I can't just ignore Scott's behavior. He'll break her heart."

"You don't know what you're talking about. Scott and Finley get along so well, a blind person could see they belong together."

"He's cheating on her, Mom."

"He wouldn't do that, and you'd know it if you took your head out of your behind and got back here where your sister needs you."

"I can't just stand around and watch Finley marry that creep."

"You'd better think about what you're doing. Your sister deserves better than this from you."

The line went dead, and I stood leaning against the post, fighting tears. The doggie door flipped open and a familiar collie trotted out and came over to me, followed closely by Scrappy. The dog sat looking up at me with big, doggie eyes. I smiled. I couldn't help it. She looked so sweet, the rat.

"Hello, Trixie."

She barked

"I'm okay. You go run for a while. Then we can talk."

She gently rubbed her head against my leg, then headed out in the yard, her kitty following right behind. Scrappy seemed to be growing every day. Maybe I should get a cat. It would be a nice companion when my family disowned me.

A few minutes later, Trixie hopped up the steps, stopped to brush her nose against me, then went through the doggie door into the house. I stayed where I was, sitting on the steps, waiting for her. Scrappy curled up beside me, I scratched the furry head, and she was soon purring. The gentle vibration was relaxing, and I was surprised how much better she made me feel.

Terri, now dressed in perfectly acceptable jeans and a red sweater, opened the door and came out. She gave Scrappy a scratch before coming around to the non-kitty side and sitting beside me on the steps. "So, what's up?"

"How much did you hear?"

"I wasn't trying to listen in."

"I know that. You can't help it that your doggie self can hear what people are saying. That's how you know I'm upset."

"Yep, dogs do hear better than humans. On the other hand, it doesn't take hearing parts of your conversation to know something's up with you. I can see it on your face."

I sighed. "Mom called, and she gave me hell for walking out on Finley's wedding preparations."

"I'm sorry."

I shrugged. "I expected it. I just don't understand how she can ignore all the times I've predicted something that came true. Dad's mother, my grandmother, did what I do. Mom even admits that sometimes. But she still insists I'm just saying this stuff to cause trouble or get something, or whatever. Now it's that I'm jealous of Finley, by the way."

"Because she has a cheating fiancé, I take it."

I laughed in spite of myself. "Yes, I have always wanted a cheating fiancé."

"You need to get out for a while. Hunter and I are going over to the house to see what needs to be done. Come with us."

"I don't want to intrude."

"Oh, trust me, you won't be intruding." She hopped up and held out her hand.

Chapter 4

I'm psychic, so I should have seen it coming. But I was so wrapped up in my own pathetic problems I didn't realize what the sneaky dog-girl was up to until I was standing in the middle of a house that badly needed an upgrade, crowbar in my hand, looking at the big smile on Terri's face.

"I told you it'd be fun," she said.

"I didn't realize tearing up a kitchen was so hard." I leaned against the nearest wall and rested the crowbar against what was left of a counter.

"Me either," Terri said. "But it's cathartic."

"Sam's going to be here in about an hour to check the structural integrity," Hunter said. "I hope that wall I've been tearing the drywall off of isn't load-bearing."

"It wouldn't be the end of the world," Terri said. "We'd just have to put up a beam."

Hunter walked over and wrapped his arms around her. "We? Because I don't think either of us has the knowledge or ability to hoist a post that weighs several hundred pounds up to the ceiling and install it without the house collapsing around us."

"We can hire somebody to do it for us."

I swear I've never seen her look as innocent as she did just then. I turned away so she wouldn't see me smile.

He chuckled. "Terri Quinn can hire somebody.

Hunter Devereux will be pinching pennies on this project."

"It's our house. It belongs to both of us. When will you get over your testosterone-fueled belief that you have to be the big money maker?"

Hunter grabbed Terri and pulled her to him for a long kiss. In deference to their privacy, I looked away. That's when I saw Logan leaning against the wall near the open front door. Even though he wore his dark sunglasses, I could tell he was looking right at me. I raised one eyebrow, and he grinned. I looked away to prevent any idea that I was flirting or something.

"Look at this, we need extra help, and help appears." Hunter headed toward the newcomer. "What did you do, Logan, blow off work for a chance to do renovation?"

Logan hadn't moved a muscle. "Who said anything about helping?"

"Me." Hunter grabbed Logan's arm and pulled him to where we were working. "It's destruction, right up your alley."

"Ha ha." But he took the crowbar I'd been using and began tearing off the side of a cabinet.

Terri and I left the men to the kitchen demolition, and we went into the living room to strip off some seriously ugly, baby diaper green wallpaper.

A couple of hours later, we'd finished the wallpaper. I probably should have made up an excuse to leave, but somehow I got conned into tearing the pink tile off the wall of the single bathroom. Terri worked with me for a while, then got pulled away to discuss the bearing of loads with Hunter and the Sam dude. I wasn't alone long, though. I knew who was there because some perverse part of me warmed and melted.

Logan began tearing off the tile on the other side of the room, so as we worked, we moved closer. I ignored him and kept working until a little piece of tile flew up and hit me on the face just below my safety goggles. It stung, but I didn't think much of it until something ran down my cheek and a big drop of red hit the floor. I pulled off my gloves as I looked for something to staunch the bleeding.

"Are you okay?"

The sound of actual concern in Logan's voice jumped my gaze to him. "Fine, just need something to clean up my mess."

"What happened?"

I sighed. "That tile objected to removal."

He ignored my attempt at levity, put his tools down, jerked off his safety goggles, and examined my wound. "I can't tell how bad it is because of all the blood. I'll think I saw some first aid supplies in the kitchen." He put his arm around me and edged me firmly down the hall.

"It really isn't that bad." I reached up to wipe at the warmth running down my cheek.

Logan grabbed my hand. "Don't touch that."

I looked at my grubby hands and realized he was right.

In the kitchen, Logan pulled his gloves off, squirted his hands with hand sanitizer, then grabbed paper towels from a roll I hadn't even noticed. He cleaned his hands thoroughly, then got a fresh paper towel and tipped up my chin so he could see the wound more clearly.

He was surprisingly gentle, wiping away the blood,

and my body responded to his touch by warming and melting into mush. "This is gonna sting."

I winced as he cleaned and applied antiseptic to the injury, then put a bandage on my cheek. "Thank you."

"You're welcome." He didn't move back, just stood there looking deep into my eyes. "I'd hate for that sweet face to be scarred."

My breath caught in my chest, and I froze, looking into his eyes. They were deep brown with bits of green and blue and yellow. I found myself caught up in the depths of his gaze, where I saw warmth and caring. Not something I'd have ever imagined lurked there.

He leaned toward me, and I told myself to back away. My brain must have been confused because instead of taking a step back, my stupid body leaned toward him. He slipped his arms around me and smiled as he moved in to cover my lips with his.

He tasted like warm cinnamon and spicy male. I moaned a little as I wondered how I had survived this long without knowing how wonderful a man could make me feel.

The kiss was long, slow, through, and so hot I'm pretty sure my panties smoked by the time he let up. We pulled apart slowly.

He slowly licked his lips and whispered, "Yum."

"Oh, sorry," somebody said.

Still dizzy from the encounter, I looked in the direction of the speaker. Terri stood watching us and not looking in the least bit sorry.

"A piece of tile hit Dia in the face." Logan indicated the bandage on my cheek.

"So you were kissing her to make it all better?"

He grinned. "Yes, I was. Did it work, sweetheart?"

Sweetheart? "Um, yeah, thanks, Logan."

Terri rolled her eyes.

A knock had us looking toward the open kitchen door.

"Sorry if I'm interrupting." The man standing in the doorway was tall, thin, and had long gray hair pulled straight back into a ponytail that hung halfway down his back. He was wearing patched jeans and a worn black T-shirt with Bela Lugosi as Dracula on the front. "I saw y'all working over here and thought I'd stop by to say howdy." He held out his hand. "My name is Arlo. I'm your neighbor from across the street, the brown house with the big tree out front."

"You're not interrupting." She shook Arlo's hand. "I'm Terri, and that's my fiancé Hunter." She pointed to the man who had just come from the living room where the two of them had been working.

"And this is Dia and Logan, they're helping us with the renovation."

"Good to meet you," Arlo said. "I was hoping somebody would buy this place and fix it up. It's got good bones, but the last owners weren't big on keeping things in pristine condition."

"How long have you lived in this neighborhood?" Hunter asked as he too shook the man's hand.

"About fifteen years. It's a nice place to be, and I've loved every minute since I moved in."

We spent the next few minutes talking to the new neighbor. People in Ugly Creek tended to be more than they seemed. And Arlo was not your average old hippie type. I didn't touch him, so I can't give specifics, but there was a lot this guy wasn't saying. I hoped I had a chance to get to know him better. Now wasn't the time, though. I was tired and in serious need of a shower. At that moment, my stomach reminded me I hadn't eaten in hours.

"How about we go get some dinner? I'll bring you back later to get your car."

Dinner? Apparently, we'd been working longer than I thought. "I rode with Terri and Hunter."

Logan moved to my side, brushed my hair back, and proceeded to examine my ear.

"What do you think you're doing?"

"Looking for a gullible bug."

Bug? Yikes! "You're looking for a what?"

"A gullible bug."

I stared at him, and he tipped his head to the side and looked right back.

"You're an intelligent woman who doesn't strike me as someone to fall for a trick like riding with a couple, so you'd be stuck helping them until they decided to take you back home. Therefore, you must have been slipped a gullible bug."

He made as if to pull something out of my ear, toss it on the floor, and stomped hard. "There you go. You're all safe from the ugly gullible bug for now, but don't let Devereux anywhere near your head. He's a devious one."

"You're nuts. You know that?"

Logan grinned. "Ah sugar, you say the sweetest things."

I laughed, but not for long. His accent was exaggerated, but like Hunter's, it was real. Odd, I'd have pegged him as a Yankee snob, but he was a Southern boy.

He had a crazy sense of humor too, and he'd been

gentle and caring with me. I didn't want to admit it, but there was more depth to Logan Montgomery than I'd ever considered possible. Excitement deep inside me tingled at the possibility of breaking through his barriers and getting to know the many layers the man kept hidden inside.

He put an arm around me as we headed over to where the other three talked about renovation like it was the most interesting subject in the entire world.

"I'm stealing your poor, starving guest," Logan said.

Terri bit her lower lip and cringed. "I'm sorry, Dia, I hadn't even thought about food. I guess Hunter and I maybe got a little too caught up in our new project."

"We appreciate both of you helping us out," Hunter said, his expression an appropriate shade of shame.

"No problem, man," Logan said. "Maybe we'll even do it again. If you supply refreshments. "

Terri abruptly wrapped me in a bear hug. "See you at home," she leaned close and whispered in my ear. "I won't wait up."

"Okay," I whispered back, my face warm from the implication.

She let go, and Logan put his arm around me again. Together we walked out to his car.

****

We were too dirty to go into a restaurant, so we grabbed drive-through sandwiches and went to Logan's apartment.

His place wasn't large. It was a tiny section inside a smallish rectangular building that had likely started as a business of some kind before it was cut up into small apartments. The front door opened into a living room furnished in mid-twentieth century beige.

We walked through the living room into the white kitchen and put our food on the blue Formica topped table. The apartment was small, the furniture old, but clean. It didn't look like anything a bad boy would bring his women home to.

"Not bad." I was careful not to look at him as I spoke.

"The company sublet some apartments for us to stay in while we're in Ugly Creek. They came furnished."

I grinned. "That explains your 'granny's Aunt Matilda' choice of decor."

He winced. "Have you ever thought about doing comedy?"

"Yes, but every time I mention the idea, somebody laughs in my face."

He smiled as he touched his fingertips to my cheek. "You know, most people share apartments to cut cost, but I decided I valued my privacy. There was this place where the so-called second bedroom is the size of a closet. And not a walk-in closet either." He smiled, and the room got brighter. "So we won't be interrupted if you want to practice your comedy routine. Or whatever."

I ignored the "whatever" remark. "It's nice, Logan, and I understand needing your own space. I need to work on that back home."

"You share an apartment?"

I nodded my cheek warming by the second from his touch. "With my sister. She wanted a place closer to town, and it seemed logical that we could afford a more expensive place."

"So it was what your sister wanted, not you?"

I shrugged. "Like I said, it made sense."

"Closer to her work?"

I shrugged. "Yes."

"And your work?"

I shrugged. "Maybe a little farther away."

"So you share an apartment, so your sister can have the place she wants."

I held up my hands in surrender. "Okay, so I'm a pushover. But I've learned that giving in to my strong-willed sister is easier on the nerves."

Logan studied my face for a moment, then moved my hair so he could look into my ear. "There must be more gullible bugs in here."

I shook my head in consternation. "There you go with the bug thing again."

"There has to be an explanation for your actions."

"There is. My sister is a pain."

He moved, so our faces were inches apart. "You know you are allowed to say no."

I considered my stubborn sister, then sighed. "Trust me, with Finley, It's easier to just go along with her."

Abruptly he grabbed me and pulled me against him. "You are too big-hearted for your own good."

My face went hot, and in spite of myself, I giggled. "If you say so."

He tipped up my chin, so we were looking into each other's eyes, "I say so."

His were dark and inviting. I felt I could just fall in there. What would it be like, to float around in those beautiful pools? I reached up and touched his face.

He put his hand over mine, pressing me gently against his cheek. Slowly he moved closer, gently, carefully covering my mouth with his. He tasted spicy, warm, yummy.

"You're a sweet, giving person." He kept his hands on my shoulders as he backed up. "I'll bet people take advantage of you on a regular basis."

I really wanted to tell him he was wrong, but he wasn't. My cheeks warmed, so I lowered my head, and focused on not showing my embarrassment.

"You should turn and run away from me. I'm not the kind of man a sweetheart like you should be hanging around with."

I met his gaze and held it. "I know."

"You aren't running."

"I've never been one to do what was expected of me."

He leaned toward me again, his warm, firm lips touching mine. His arms held me against him, sending warm tingles down my spine. My arms slid around him, and I basked in the experience.

And then my stomach let out a loud growl.

I closed my eyes and leaned my forehead against Logan's chest, totally humiliated.

"Why don't we eat," he said.

I kept my head down as I nodded my agreement. He snagged me with an arm around my waist and pulled me back against him.

"Food is a basic human need, like sleep, and…"He paused for a moment, leaned close, and whispered, "sex."

I held on hard to my amusement, but when I saw the twinkle in his eyes, I lost the fight. He followed suit, and we laughed until we were both red in the face.

We sat at the table and dined on our greasy

burgers, Afterward, he took me to Terri's aunt's house. The whole time, he acted like a perfect gentleman.

And I didn't believe it for a second.

Chapter 5

Terri was once again writing—late for her—when I walked into the kitchen. Though the sun had barely topped the mountains, Hunter had made coffee. I poured myself a cup and joined him at the kitchen table. He was frowning at his laptop, and I couldn't resist teasing him a little.

"Keep that up, and you'll burn a hole right through your hard work."

"Not so much hard work as having a hard time digesting what I just found out."

"You're working on a book about Ugly Creek, right? "

He nodded.

"If you didn't find something weird around every corner, I'd be worried about you."

He chuckled, "Isn't that the truth? It's doubly strange, though, because what I found is about our next-door neighbor."

"Ms. Carlisle?"

"The very same. You know her husband suddenly disappeared?"

"Terri told me about that. He just vanished, apparently took off to get away from her."

"Except there was nothing to prove he'd left. Nobody saw him in or leaving town. There were no charges on his credit cards, no withdrawals from their joint bank account, no sightings anywhere."

Interest swirled in me, and I came around the table to see what he was looking at. He opened an article about the disappearance of one Darin Carlisle. His wife was mentioned as a "person of interest".

Then Hunter pulled up an email. "This is from Ken Bennett with the Ugly Creek Police Department."

Even after what Hunter had said and reading the article, it was still unnerving to read what the police officer said in the email, "They believed he was dead, and she was the number one suspect?"

"She's still the number one suspect. The case was never closed."

"But she wasn't charged?"

"No body, no blood, no specific evidence connecting Mrs. C to the disappearance of Mr. C."

Footsteps announced the arrival of Terri. "I was working my butt off while the two of you gossip about our neighbor." Terri crossed her arms and looked at the two of us as if we were misbehaving children.

"It's not gossip if it's true," I pointed out.

"Bull," she shot back. "So, what's up with the crazy cat woman?"

"She's the number one suspect in her husband's disappearance," Hunter said.

Terri whistled softly. "Dang, I know she's a loony old bat, but I never thought she might be a murderer."

"It tracks with what your dad said," Hunter said.

Terri nodded. "It does, doesn't it?"

I didn't want to stick my nose where it didn't belong, but my curiosity was killing me. "What did your dad say?"

I caught her slight shiver. "His canine half smelled

human decomposition in her flower bed."

****

The video was of five white-coated people sitting around a large table. An older man, wearing a labcoat over a suit and tie, came into view and sat at the head of the table."You are all doing a wonderful job," he said. "I really appreciate the work you are doing, and I believe we can get patents for several new products and processes.

He leaned forward, his metal-rimmed glasses magnifing the eyes with which he regarded first one person, then another. "However, let's be sure to keep our eyes on the big prize."

He looked over the camera for a moment, then went on to the next person. "Ultimitely, we are here for one thing, and one thing only."

"Yes, sir!" Voices soounded around the table.

"Good deal. Now get back to work."

He left, and the rest wasted no time following him out.

****

"That wall has to be taken down." Terri's voice cut through the house, out an open window, and caught me right in the growing headache.

"Can't we work around it somehow ?" Exasperation permeated Hunter's voice.

I felt for the man. When Terri decides on a course of action, woe to the person who got in her way.

"All we need to do is put in a support beam."

"And you'll pay for it?" Hunter's voice rose with every word.

"Why not?"

I did my best to ignore the bickering couple as I

walked around to the other end of their house and outside. I didn't want to hear them. It wasn't my business.

A yellow car parked at the edge of the road, and tingles crawled up my spine as Logan got out and strode my way.

"How long have they been at it?" he asked.

"Long enough to make me very uncomfortable."

He put his arms around me, and tugged me closer. "Run away with me. Leave that crazy couple to their project, and I'll buy you a delicious dinner somewhere cheap."

"Well, aren't you the gentleman?"

"No." He looked into my eyes. "No, I'm not. I did say cheap, remember."

I looked up at him, feeling my logic circuit twitching. I should be turning tail and running, but that was not what I wanted to do. Not at all. What I wanted was to stand there and look up into gorgeous eyes for the rest of forever.

Then he leaned toward me. Slowly. Anticipation grew as he moved, as he came closer and touched his lips to mine. He was gentle, but there was a fire underneath that both warmed me and made me fear getting burned.

When he pulled away, my hands grabbed his shirt. I forced my fingers to let go,

"You taste so good," he whispered.

I just stood there, staring up at him like a lovesick puppy.

"They've stopped fighting."

What was he talking about? "Oh, okay," I muttered.

"We could go help them." He tucked a lock of my hair behind my ear. "Or we could just kiss some more."

That sounded so good I was about to grab him and get started. Unfortunately before I could, footsteps came toward us.

"What are you two doing out here? We could really use you inside."

Logan leaned his forehead against mine as he sighed. "What do you think?

That we should tell Hunter to go away. "That's what I came here for," I said.

"Me too, but that's not what I want."

'We're putting up drywall," Hunter said.

"They need us."

I looked into his eyes one more time, swallowed hard, and released my hold on his neck. He grinned, the scoundrel.

I shoved up my chin, forced my legs into action, and headed toward the front door.

Hunter stood nearby, his mouth twitching, clearly fighting a smile. Well, this was going to be an interesting afternoon.

****

Hours later, the waning moon beamed down on me as I sat on the back steps. Inside her aunt's house, Terri and Hunter were watching a movie. They asked me to join them, but I seriously needed time to be alone and think. My whole reason for making the trip to Tennessee was to enjoy some much-needed support from my closest friend and to get away from my crazy family. I didn't come here to find a date. The last thing I needed at the moment was a complication to my already overly-complicated life. And Logan

Montgomery was as complicated as they come.

Shoving aside the thoughts of the male pain in my neck, I considered what I'd expected to get from my trip north. I'd needed comfort and support; that was for sure. For that, nobody is better than my buddy Terri. Plus, Hunter was very nice. And Logan was amazing.

"Stop it!" I stood and wandered away from the house. Logan was not the subject of the current issues. The question was, what did I want to gain by coming to Ugly Creek? Was I just running away? Because I could be fine with that. Getting away from my nutso mom and selfish sister was enough of a reason to visit with my closest friend. Then again, visiting my friend was a fine reason to travel to Tennessee. It was great seeing her and meeting her new man. But was that the whole reason for the trip?

No. I had hoped the distance would give me some clarity, help me to understand how to deal with my sister's stubborn disbelief and my mom's denial of my ability. And, deep down, I'd hoped my leaving might shock them enough they might consider I was serious about what I'd seen. That I was honestly trying to protect my sister.

I gave my head a quick shake that was so hard the movement left a twinge in my neck. I had to face the fact that Mom and Finley would rather believe I had some ulterior motive than just accept the truth. So what now? My home was in Florida. I had a job, an apartment, a life. I truly wanted to be the maid of honor for my sister, but I couldn't just ignore what I'd seen in my vision and let her marry a man who I knew would break her heart.

I let out a big, heartfelt sigh as I leaned back

against one of the white wooden columns supporting the roof over the porch. At some point, I would have to either decide to stay in Ugly Creek or go home and deal with my disconcerting life and baffling family.

And leave Logan forever.

I wasn't sure which unsettled me the most.

A movement caught my attention. There was a hill just beyond the fence line. A thick copse of trees covered the hill, as well as wild flowers, and lush greenery. And apparently I'd seen the movement of some small animal.

Then, by one of the trees, I saw what looked like a very large person. I squinted to see better. Whatever was up there moved away from the tree, turned and walked away. At the very top of the hill, it stood for a moment. I saw it clearly in the moonlight. Its arms were too long; its body proportions were wrong. And there was fur covering its body. The creature looked back, and I felt that it knew I was there. One big hand lifted as if waving, then it turned and went down the other side.

Total shock held me for a moment. Then I grinned. They did exist.

How awesome!

Chapter 6

"I will not leave my best friend alone. Not when she's here for love and support." Terri wrapped her arms around me and hugged me so hard I couldn't breathe.

"She's turning purple," Hunter said.

Terri looked at me, released her grip, and propped her fists on her hips. "You humans are too easy to break."

"Doggie's too strong," I gasped.

"I'm sorry."

I gave her a narrow-eyed glare. "That's why you're grinning?"

"Admit it. You love me anyway."

Her expression was so innocent and sweet I almost started laughing. I caught Hunter's gaze. "How do you put up with her?"

"Hey!"

Hunter shrugged. "What can I say? I love the crazy woman."

Terri rubbed against him like a puppy looking for love. "And dog."

He pulled her close. "And dog." Then he kissed her long and thoroughly.

"When you two finish, please go do your thing on the reno house."

They turned to look at me.

"Are you sure?" Hunter asked. "I can go by myself and Terri can stay here. Maybe you can watch a chick flick or something."

"Yes, I'm sure."

A half-hour later, Terri and Hunter had gone to work on their house, and I was wandering alone through the town of Ugly Creek. The weather was mild for early March, and I was enjoying the walk.

As before, I could sense history permeating the area. I could almost see visions as I looked around, but the images weren't quite strong enough. I wondered why that happened here and not in other old places. Probably because Ugly Creek wasn't your average town, old or not.

I turned a corner, and the utilitarian block building across the road shook me out of my musings. I glanced toward the parking lot, and there was the familiar yellow car. Logan was there, working for the company that had set up a lab for whatever they were doing in Ugly Creek. I didn't trust big companies, and that distrust extended to those who worked for them. Like the enigmatic Logan Montgomery.

I crossed the street and wandered around a bit, trying to check things out without letting on about what I was doing.

In the back were lunch tables and a couple of big, blue metal trash cans. I caught movement and a familiar figure leaned against a tree.

Logan was fiddling with a pack of cigarettes. Yuck. Nasty habit and another reason not to like the man. Odd though that I hadn't smelled them on him.

He pulled a cigarette out of the pack and stared at it for a time. He put it in his mouth, then pulled it back out like it bit him.

Well, that was weird. I waited a minute to see what else he would do. Mostly he just glared at the vile things. After a few minutes, curiosity got the best of me, and I walked toward him as quietly as I could.

"I didn't know you smoked."

He jumped like a teenage boy caught with a girly magazine. "You scared me."

"Sorry," I lied.

He stared at the package in his hand. "I don't. Well, I did, but I quit a few years ago." He wadded the cigarettes into a ball and tossed it into the big metal trash can. "Thank you for reminding me I'm capable of handling stress without reverting to burning paper-covered weeds in my mouth."

"I didn't do anything. I just happened to pass by."

Logan took my hands in his. "Just looking at you makes me feel more relaxed and happy."

My face went hot. "I had no idea I could have that kind of effect."

"For me, you do."

I realized just then that Logan had the most amazing smile I'd ever seen on any man. Ever. "How long did you smoke?"

"Almost ten years."

Shock skittered through me, and I gasped. "You must have started young."

He wiggled his eyebrows. "Either that or I'm a lot older than you thought."

I bit back the smile. "So you're actually eighty-five?"

His lips twitched, but he held a straight face. "How did you guess?"

"I'm psychic."

"Ha ha."

I poked the toe of my sandal at a clump of grass. "Obviously, I was teasing about your age, but I am psychic."

He narrowed his eyes at me. "What am I thinking?"

I resigned myself to whatever came next. "It doesn't work that way."

"How does it work?"

I looked into his eyes. Was he teasing me? Oh, what the hell? "When I touch a person, I get pictures in my head.

"Visions."

I nodded, gauging his reaction as I did. "Sometimes just a picture, sometimes there are sounds, or smells, or strong feelings."

"Sounds interesting." He gently edged me over to one of the nearby benches. I sat, and without moving his hand from my back, he took a seat beside me.

"It can be interesting, but sometimes it causes problems."

He winced. "I can imagine."

Again I studied his face. Was he that open to the idea of a person being psychic?

"Are your visions always from the past?"

I shook my head, holding his gaze as I did. "It can be past, present, or future."

"How do you know which is which?"

I couldn't believe that Logan wasn't making fun of me or telling me psychic phenomena were the result of my imagination. "Wait," I said. "You believe me?"

His forehead tightened, revealing small lines I'd

have thought him too young to have.

"Why wouldn't I believe you?"

I shrugged. "You're a scientist, and I've been told many times that science proves psychics are deluded or scammers out to rip off little old people."

He brushed a lock of hair off my face, leaving a warm trail where he touched me. "That's funny because scientists have studied psychic phenomena for over a hundred years."

"And found nothing."

A little smile pulled at his lips as he slowly shook his head. "That's not exactly true. Both the U.S. and Russia have had successful trials using people who tested high on PSI tests. A lot of the specifics are still classified, but I know at least some of them worked. There are rumors that the CIA makes use of psychic visions to this day."

My heart slammed against my chest as I studied Logan's beautiful eyes. "You're making that up."

"No. Honest, I've seen the data."

"I thought that was something to sell books and cheesy cable shows."

He shook his head. "The government would prefer if we all believed that, but the truth is most of us don't know just how we, or the Russians, used the things they learned. Or how they're still using them."

"You're serious."

He used a finger to shove my chin up and close my mouth. "I'm not as stodgy and boring as my buddy Hunter." He looked away and licked his lips. "I've heard how hard it was for poor Terri to get through to the stubborn nerd." He met my gaze again. "Terri and Trixie."

I swallowed. Did he mean what I think he did? I decided to poke around a little. "About how close the two of them are?"

He nodded slowly. "How he had to accept both of them."

"You know what she is, don't you?"

He tipped his head to one side. "Let's see, gorgeous female."

My breath caught, and a wave of something that might be jealousy washed over me.

"And she's also half-human."

The laughter blew out of me like air out of a popped balloon.

"Since you're her best friend, I was pretty certain you knew her secret, but I didn't want just to blurt it out."

"I'm glad. It means you respect her privacy."

So he wasn't as bad as I thought? Maybe.

"Could I take you to lunch?"

"Don't you have to get back to work?"

"Yes, but if I don't take some time, I'll tell my boss a few things that would probably end my career."

"That bad?"

"Worse." He held out his hand. "Let's go get food."

We ate burgers at a tiny place that had just opened a block from the building where he worked. For most of the meal, there was little conversation, and what there was centered around topics like the weather, how beautiful Ugly Creek was, and what a cute couple Terri and Hunter were. Then Logan changed directions.

"You said you can tell the difference between visions of the past, present, and future events. I'm intrigued. Would you mind sharing?"

He was actually interested. Nobody but Terri had ever asked about how what I did worked.

"Present feels like it's happening as I watch. That's what I usually get. Visions from the past are kinda smoky or blurry. Future events are the least common, and they're kind of like looking through the wrong end of binoculars."

"That's pretty interesting."

"You think so?"

He nodded. "I do. So, what do you feel when you touch me?"

I took a sip of my drink to give myself a moment to think. "I don't get visions when I touch you."

"So, there are some people you don't get anything from."

"Well, actually…" I seriously needed to learn to lie.

He leaned back and studied me. "Wait, are you saying it's just me? That I'm the only person, you don't get visions from?"

I poked at what was left of my burger. "Yes."

The touch of his hand grasping mine had me looking at him again. "You aren't getting anything?" he asked.

I closed my eyes and tried to reach out into whatever mystical place my visions came from. Nothing.

I shook my head. "Sorry."

He leaned back in his seat, my hand still clasped in his. "So this has never happened with any of your…um…male friends?"

"No." I poked at my burger again. "Not that I've had a lot of experience, but there doesn't seem to be a difference between gender, or my relationship with the person." My face heated as I met Logan's gaze. "Honestly, it worried me a lot until I realized there wasn't a difference."

"Thought you'd see things you didn't want to, huh?"

"I had no idea what I'd find out. Like it's not scary enough getting to know a guy." I realized what I'd said, and my face went from hot to burn.

"Do I scare you?"

I forced myself to look at him. "A little."

He leaned toward me and put his free hand against my cheek. "I would never hurt you."

I nodded as I looked down at my food again.

His fingertip edged my chin back up. "I get that you haven't known me long enough to trust me, but if you give me a chance, I'll work hard to prove myself."

It was easy to smile as I thought about ways he could go about proving his trustworthiness to me.

"Why do I have the feeling that proving myself won't be easy?"

Unexpected happiness bubbled up inside of me. This man was fun, caring, attentive, and he hadn't dismissed my ability.

"If it were easy, you wouldn't really be showing me that I can trust you."

"I'll give you that."

We walked hand-in-hand back to where I first saw Logan. We were almost there when a voice from behind us startled me.

"Well, Mr. Montgomery. Now I understand why you aren't in a hurry to get back to work."

Logan's hand tightened on mine before he let go,

and we turned to face the man behind us. "Dia Grey, this is my boss, Dr. Miles Lynch. Doctor, this is my friend Dia."

The man was well-dressed and handsome. The smile, wire-rimmed glasses and a touch of gray in his sideburns created a picture of a man who could be trusted. "It's nice to meet you, Ms. Grey," he said as he held out his hand.

I met his grip with my own, and any good feeling I'd had seconds ago vanished. I knew without a doubt that this man could *not* be trusted. In fact, the pictures that sifted through my mind were filled with greed and a lack of empathy. The coarseness of his thoughts was so strong and unexpected that I swayed.

"Are you all right there, young lady?"

I stepped back and put a hand on my forehead. "Yes, I...um... have an inner ear thing that throws my balance off if I don't take my medication." I forced a smile. "I just realized I forgot to take my pills this morning. Sorry."

Dr. Lynch's eyes slightly narrowed, and his jaw tightened. He wasn't buying it. Logan slid his arm around my shoulders and leaned close.

"It's my fault," Logan said. "I called you this morning."

My face heated at the very thought of Logan's deep voice calling first thing in the morning. "You are rather distracting sometimes."

He leaned close and whispered just loud enough that his boss likely heard too. "I could hear you blush through the line."

My face felt so hot it might catch my hair on fire. "Proud of yourself, are you Montgomery?"

He grinned. "Oh yeah, I sure am."

I nailed his ribs with my elbow, glancing toward his boss as I did. The man was buying our play. Good.

"Dr. Lynch, would it be a problem if I drove Dia home? I don't think she should drive right now."

"Of course not, Logan. Just don't take too long."

"I won't."

He wrapped his arm around me, and I stumbled a little as we walked to his car. The stumble, of course, was just an act and had nothing to do with the sexy man whose body rubbed against mine. Not at all.

We got into Logan's yellow monster, and I was shocked at how smooth and quiet the thing ran. He drove a few minutes, then turned onto a dirt road. He went a little further, then pulled over, and turned off the motor.

"You're pretty slick with that inner ear thing."

I shrugged. "Years of practice."

"So, what did you see when you touched him?"

"I didn't really see much. It was more of a feeling."

"What kind of feeling?"

He took my hand in his, and his warmth moved through me like a sip of hot chocolate in winter. "Greed, narcissism, a need to control."

Logan sighed. "Yeah, that'd be him all right."

"How can you work with a man like that?" I immediately wanted to take back my words. "I'm sorry."

"It's okay. You're such a sweetheart, so honest and caring. I guess it's a good thing you can't read me."

"You aren't anything like him."

His face went dark, and his laugh was empty and hard. "Honey, I grew up with nothing, and I've spent my entire life trying to change that."

"You have. You're a scientist. You help change the world."

He met my gaze, and the sadness in his eyes tore my heart. "Dia, I work for a company that is only trying to change the world so the top dogs can get richer."

I shook my head and squeezed his. "You don't have to read minds to know you're a good person."

His laugh was bitter. "I appreciate your faith, but I'm not who you think I am."

"Yes, you are," I whispered.

A smile pulled at his lips. "You see into people, and yet you believe the best."

"You heard what I said about your boss."

Logan shrugged. "You were shaken by what you saw. You can't see into me, or you'd probably jump out of this car and run for your life."

I caught a glint of humor in his eyes, and I grabbed at it. "Then I guess we need to get to know each other."

He narrowed his eyes. "You think so?"

"I do."

"Okay, I'm game. What do you want to do?"

"Tomorrow's Saturday. If you're not working, we could go on a picnic."

He chuckled. "I tell you I'm not the guy you think I am, and you want to go on a picnic?"

"What better way to get to know somebody?"

"I guess I could pick up some chicken or something."

"Sounds good. I'll bring some colas."

"I'll pick you up at noon?"

I considered. "Make it eleven. We'll have time to talk and relax and still help Terri and Hunter at their house."

"Feeling guilty, huh?"

"Unfortunately, yes."

"Eleven it is." He looked at his watch. "I'd better take you home so I can go back to work."

"Yes, you should. I'd hate for you to have problems with that narcissistic boss of yours."

Logan sighed. "I agree with you there, though I'm beginning to think it might be inevitable."

"Why would you say that?"

"He's a jerk."

"But he's still your boss."

"Yeah." Logan dropped his head against the steering wheel. "That being the conundrum."

I put my hand on his shoulder. "Maybe I'm totally out of touch, but couldn't you find a job somewhere else? Somewhere that pays well, but the boss isn't such a grumpy head."

Logan raised an eyebrow. "Grumpy head?"

I nodded. "Grumpy head."

"You're something else. You know that?"

"Yes, I do."

He sighed. "Thing is, very few jobs pay as much as the one I have."

"So?"

He locked gazes with me. "So, money is important."

I tilted my head to change my view. "More important than the earth where we live? Or the people who care about you?"

"You've obviously always had enough money for whatever you needed or wanted. Not everyone is that lucky."

I looked at him then and truly saw him for the first time. Designer clothes, flashy car, expensive haircut, arrogant attitude, dark sunglasses hiding eyes that might reveal something he didn't want anybody to know, like insecurity.

"Maybe I had more money, but that doesn't mean I had what I needed. There are things that are more important than clothes or cars, or even food and housing."

"Oh, really?"

I so wanted to smack the condescension out of his voice. "Yes, really. Now, if you would take me home, please."

He lifted a hand and seemed to start to say something, but then the hand dropped to his lap, and he sighed long and hard. "I'm sorry, Dia. Honest. I guess getting defensive might be an indication that I'm not totally comfortable with the idea of putting money before everything else."

Well, this was interesting. "So why do you put money first?"

He poked at the steering wheel for a moment. "Because money changes things."

"Like power?"

He shot me a sharp glance. "Respect."

"Things," I shot back. "Nice, expensive things."

His jaw clenched, and his eyes narrowed. "No worrying about where your next meal is coming from."

That stopped me for a moment. Wow! Then I considered the situation. "You could get that from flipping burgers." I held his gaze. "Or working for a nicer boss."

Logan leaned his head back against the seat. "So I

like nice things." His gaze connected with mine again. "Really nice things."

"Nice things that are worth working for a grumpy head?"

He held up his hands as if in surrender. "Okay, I admit you've given me a few things to think about."

"Good."

He chuckled. "Still on for tomorrow?"

"Absolutely."

"Then I'd better get you home and get back to work before Grumpy head tears me to pieces and feeds me to the ducks."

A few minutes later, we were at my temporary home.

"I'll get a buddy of mine to help me, and we'll bring your car home." He walked me to the door, touched his lips gently against mine, then headed back toward town.

I wouldn't admit it to him, but he'd given me some things to think about too

* * * *

The video shook and jerked at times, but it clearly showed the anger on the face of a lab-coated man with metal-rimmed glasses.

"Damn it!" the man said. "Are you sure you actually saw one?"

A skinny guy, who looked like he was still a teenager, was pulling a lab coat on. "Yes, sir, it was approximately ten meters away and partially obscured by a tree, but I'm sure."

And you didn't shoot it?"

"By the time I was sure what it was, it was gone." He shifted uncomfortably. "Montgomery was there too."

The man shifted his gaze closer to the camera. "You didn't shoot it either."

"I didn't get a good look at whatever it was. It could have been a bear."

"You know it wasn't." the skinny guy said.

"Sorry, but from my perspctive I couldn't really see the creature."

"Next time, shoot first, worry if it's a bear later. Got it?"

"Yes, sir," two voices answered.

The older man snorted through his nose like an angry bull as he exited the room.

Chapter 7

I stepped out into the chilly air, drenched in sweat in spite of the spring temperatures. The cool felt wonderful to my overheated body, but when I closed my eyes, I saw the same pattern I'd been seeing for the last few hours. One thing was for sure, I never wanted to see another piece of ugly wallpaper as long as I lived.

Then I grinned. Terri and I had kicked that ugly wallpaper's butt. Not a sliver of the puke green and sick yellow stuff remained on the wall of her soon-to-be dining room. I was drained but happy to feel the zing of accomplishment.

The familiar voice caught my attention, and I moved slowly toward the sound. I didn't want to invade Logan's privacy, but I wanted to know if he'd gotten in trouble with his boss.

Okay, there was also a strong need to see him, look into his eyes, and make sure I hadn't dreamed his earlier acceptance of my ability.

I stepped around the corner to the rear of the house, and he stood with his back to me, his cell phone to his ear. I started to go toward him until I heard what he was saying.

"Yes, sir. I understand. The last thing I want is for somebody else to get tied up in this mess. Especially her."

I tried to move back stealthily, but I stepped on a

stick, and the snapping sound caught Logan's attention. He swung around, both hands up and knees slightly bent, almost like a fighter readying for battle. For a second, we both froze, then he let out a long breath.

"Call you later." He clicked off his phone and shoved it into his back pocket. "Dia."

I forced a smile. "Hi, Logan. Sorry, I didn't realize you were busy." I started to turn back the way I came.

"Don't go."

"It's okay, really. I should probably get back in there and help Terri." Maybe some work would make me feel less guilty for the spying.

"Are we still on for tomorrow?"

I shrugged. "I hope so."

"If you still want to go on a picnic, I have an old blanket in the car we could use."

I grinned. "Sure, an old dirty blanket. Sounds romantic for sure."

He grinned back. "It's clean. It's just old. I keep it in my car in case I need to put something in there that might mess up the upholstery or something."

"Like Trixie?"

He looked up toward the top of the house and attempted an innocent look on his face. "Maybe once I was called on to pick the dog up at the groomers. Hunter had an appointment to dig for old dirt."

"Old dirt, huh? And you keep the blanket ready just in case?"

"Okay, he was in search of historical information. And I kinda thought it might be a good idea to keep a blanket ready in case I got asked on a picnic by a beautiful woman."

"Sounds like a perfectly logical reason." A cool

breeze brushed my still damp body, and I shivered. Damn, I was so hot inside I never considered bringing my sweater out with me.

"You're cold." Logan walked toward me, sliding out of his jacket as he moved. When he got close enough, he wrapped the warm jacket around me then followed with his arms, pulling me close and holding me against his body.

"How come you're so warm?"

He chuckled. "No clue. Just always been that way."

I looked up at him, and he kissed my forehead, then tucked my head under his chin. "You need a sweater or something."

"I have one. It's in the house."

"Well, that's not helpful."

"I know. I got hot working in there."

He leaned back a little and looked into my eyes. "You need to take care of yourself." He leaned close, his lips just brushing mine. "Or maybe you need somebody to take care of you."

"Are you volunteering?"

He shrugged. "Don't know. What do you think of the idea?"

"I've heard worse."

He touched his lips to mine and slowly, softly, carefully deepened the kiss. He pulled me in so slowly that I wasn't even aware of what he was doing until he'd taken total possession of my mouth, and my body ached for him to do the same to the rest of me.

"And I thought they were going to help us." Hunter's voice came from the corner of the house.

Logan's lips lifted in a smile, but he didn't stop the attention he was giving to my mouth, and back, and waist, and—

"Logan!"

He chuckled, the varmint. "Anybody ever told you that you have an amazing butt?"

My face went scalding hot. "No."

He kissed his way from my mouth to my ear. "Amazing," he breathed while he gently squeezed my behind.

"I think we lost them," Terri said.

"Maybe we should join them."

Hunter's voice had deepened, or at least I thought it had. I glanced their way and found the other couple joined by the mouth and one of Terri's long legs wrapped around Hunter.

"Maybe we should go while we have the opportunity."

"But we said we would help them."

Logan took my face in his hands. "We have. I've been here three hours, and you were here before me. It's time to relax and enjoy ourselves." His stomach growled. "I rest my case."

"Okay, let's go before your stomach turns into a bear and eats me."

"Ha ha." He kissed me again, and I would have followed him to the ends of the earth.

Chapter 8

The morning sunlight shining through the windows stirred happiness deep inside me. Or was it remembering how much fun the delicious Logan and I had over dinner?

"I can't believe the two of you like that nasty acidic stuff." Terri took a long sip of her drink and closed her eyes. "This is the way to start your day, with a smooth, sweet cup of tea.'"

Hunter shot her a look over the rim of his cup. "Can't beat coffee for waking up in the morning."

"Some of us don't need help getting up in the morning," she shot back.

Hunter stuck out his tongue at her.

I didn't quite hold in the laugh, and they both looked at me.

"Sorry. The two of you are just so cute."

"Bite me," Terri said.

The knock kept me from having to think of a comeback. Terri headed toward the door, and I sat back to enjoy my morning drink.

"Aunt Octavia," Terri said, and my coffee was forgotten as I rushed toward the living room.

"I've come to see your friend." Aunt Octavia smiled at me. "Dia has asked for guidance with her gift, and I'm here to offer my assistance.

Pure shock blew through me. "I didn't ask. I just

thought about how much you could teach me and how little I actually know about my ability."

"First lesson," Aunt Octavia took my hands in hers as she spoke. "Your thoughts, especially if you feel strongly about those thoughts, are picked up by the energies that are the basis of everything. These energies want the best for you, so they'll try hard to give you what you're imagining."

"So I simply thought about how nice it would be to have you for a teacher, and you got the message to come and offer your services?"

Aunt Octavia laughed. "Not exactly, but there is some truth in that."

I closed my eyes for a moment; the better to consider all this new information. "In other words, I have a lot to learn."

"Bingo."

"Which kind of proves the adage, be careful what you ask for." Terri said.

"Exactly." Auntie O grinned from ear to ear. "All right then, let's get started."

****

I was still feeling a little shaken by the morning's lesson as Logan, and I strolled down a path leading through a copse of maple and oak trees. The weather was cool enough to be uncomfortable, but since we were moving, it wasn't bad at all. Being alone with Logan in such a beautiful setting was amazing. I felt like I could stay here with him forever.

All at once, we came out of the trees at the edge of a field. Dotting the area were purple, yellow, and white wildflowers, and butterflies fluttered between them. I stood there, entranced by the beauty around us.

"I take it this is the place?"

I smiled. "Looks like a good spot to me. What do you think?"

"So, you've never been here before."

I shrugged. "Terri and Hunter recommended the area. They sounded pretty excited about it."

Logan snorted. "Doesn't take much to excite those two."

"True, but it is pretty out here."

"Yes, it is."

He smiled my way, and my breath caught in my throat. I took a moment to suck air back into my lungs. "Regardless of who suggested this place, I think it's a perfect spot for our picnic."

"I agree."

We spread a blanket on the ground, and I discovered he'd not only brought the promised chicken, but also fruit, chips, and desserts I seriously doubted we'd get around to eating. At first, we were pretty quiet, I don't know what he was feeling, but I felt relaxed and comfortable. We'd been alone together at his apartment, but out in the middle of nowhere, it was like being in a world all our own.

"You brought enough food for an army."

He grinned. "I wanted to cover my bases."

"Bases covered."

"Do you like strawberries?"

"I love strawberries."

"Awesome." He picked a slice up and held it to my lips. Our gazes locked as the sweet berry slid into my mouth.

"Mmm, that's good!"

His lips captured mine. He took a moment to

explore, then smiled. "Definitely good."

I grabbed a grape and fed it to him. Then I discovered grape tasted good on him.

He pulled back. "We should eat."

I knew he was right, but I wanted badly to grab him and continue the game. So, we kind of did both.

A little later, I was enjoying a comfortable feeling of fullness when Logan slid toward me, took me in his arms, and kissed me like he wanted to devour me. I melted right onto the blanket. The only thing holding me in my physical form was Logan's body over mine.

"You're evil," I managed to tell him.

"Well then, you must like evil."

"Sometimes." I grinned.

A high-pitched cry grabbed my attention. I shoved him away and sat up. "Is that a baby?"

"What the hell?"

Before I even considered what I was doing, I jumped up and ran toward the sound. What the heck was going on? Had somebody left a baby out here all alone? Were the parents hurt? Had the baby been stolen?

I noticed a patch of wildflowers that seemed to be moving. There was no wind. Was this where the sound was coming from? Maybe. If so, we had to help that baby! I pushed a little harder. How long had the poor thing been out here alone?

Strong arms grabbed me from behind, abruptly halting my forward momentum. I pushed Logan, trying hard to make him release me.

"Let me go! I have to help!"

He put his mouth to my ear and whispered, "Cougars can sound like crying babies."

It took me a moment, but somewhere in the cobwebs of my brain, a memory crawled out. It was a dark night. There was the sound of a baby crying. The next day, there was much talk of a big cat wandering the area. He was right. It would be a good idea to proceed with caution. I nodded my understanding.

He kept a hand on my arm as if he didn't quite believe me. Not that I really blamed him. I'm not sure I believed myself. Slowly we moved toward the thick patch of foliage. Logan reached down for a long stick and gingerly poked at the wildflowers and shrubs.

There was more movement, and a little head emerged.

I sucked in a breath. "A baby goat. It's adorable!"

The goat was brown and white and only about three feet high from toes to the top of his fuzzy little ears.

"She is pretty cute," Logan said.

"I'm a boy!"

I backed up so fast I almost fell. I stared hard at the man beside me. "What kind of idiotic game do you think you're playing, Logan?"

"Me!"

"You're the only other person out here."

"I don't do ventriloquism."

I glared at him. "Well, somebody did."

"It wasn't me."

"Then who was it?"

He shrugged. "Like you said, the only two people out here are us."

"Well, it sure as hell wasn't me," I wasn't quite yelling. Honest.

"This is Ugly Creek, you know. Weird stuff is

pretty common around here."

"Like tiny talking goats? Give me a break." I shook; I was so mad. Why was he arguing over the impossible?

"Um, Dia …"

I stared at the creature in the flowers. "A talking baby goat? That's not possible."

"I'm not a baby, and you two are giving me a headache."

I leaned closer. "This can't be what it looks like."

"Haven't you heard?" the goat asked, "Anything can happen in Ugly Creek."

"This has to be a trick." I backed up and sat down hard.

Logan pulled me to my feet without breaking the gaze he held on the little critter. "Okay, so you can talk because it's Ugly Creek. Why are you talking to us?"

"Because I want to," the goat said.

Logan looked at me and shrugged.

"Can all the animals in Ugly Creek talk?" I asked.

"Yes." The goat gave me a smug look. "Oh, you mean English? No. Only the ones TPTB gives that power to?"

"The tipped what?" Logan asked.

"The Powers That Be, moron. TPTB."

"Did they send you to us for a reason?"

"Why would they send me to the likes of you two?"

A loud rustling of the foliage kicked my heart into high gear. Grabbing at each other's arms, Logan and I almost tripped each other as we backed away.

Behind the goat, a large turkey shoved its way through the flowers and strode right up to the furry critter. The bird immediately commenced clicking noises interspersed with loud gobbles.

"Mind your own business, Georgie," the goat said.

The turkey let out some high-pitched sounds that scraped at the nerves in my spine. It got closer to the goat, flapping its wings and making noises I would never have believed came out of a turkey.

"All right, all right," the goat said. "I'll tell them." He turned to us and said, "TPTB sent me to you two because you're supposed to be together."

There was another round of clicking and gobbling and high-pitched yelps from the turkey.

"Okay," the goat said. "And the two of you are the only ones able to hear what I say."

The turkey let out one more round of noise, then waddled away.

Goat shook his head. "That Georgie is the most annoying female I've ever met. She won't stay out of other people's business."

Personally, I was glad Georgie irritated the goat until he admitted he could only talk to us. "By the way, what's your name?" I asked, not entirely sure I wanted to know.

"Zook." The goat's chin came up, and he glared as if daring me to say anything.

"Weird name for a goat," Logan said.

"And Logan is such a great name," Zook shot back.

Logan rolled his eyes.

"And Diara," Zook continued. "That's just tiara with a D. What are you, Duh Princess?"

How did he know our names?

I leaned closer to the goat. "You are a pain in the ass."

Zook took a bite of grass and sat munching while we glared.

"What are we going to do with him?" I asked. "We can't leave him out here, and I don't know how well bringing him to Terri's aunt's would go over."

Logan raised an eyebrow. "Why can't we leave him here? We weren't the ones who brought him out into the wild. I'd be willing to bet the PT-DT thingies will take care of him."

"TPTB," Zook said. "And I'd have a little respect if I were you."

"Because," I said, "These Powers That Be apparently want him to be with us."

He gave me a look similar to the ones aimed at children who refused to go to bed until they got a cookie. "'So something out there," he waved a hand to indicate this ethereal place, "wants us to adopt this critter, and we're just going to do it, without question?"

I held his gaze. "Do you really want to leave that cute little furry thing out here?"

Logan groaned. "No."

"So, what will we do with a goat?"

"I'll take him to my rental."

Well, that was unexpected. "Isn't the company renting those rooms for their scientists? I doubt farm animals are included on the lease."

Logan shrugged. "I'm not worried about that. Let's get her over there and figure out how to make this work."

"I told you, I'm a boy."

"Okay, let's get *him* over there."

"Aren't you forgetting something?" Zook said.

"Forgetting what?" I asked.

"That I have a say in where I'm going."

" Of course you do." Logan rubbed his temples with a thumb and finger like a headache was coming on. "Okay, we feel the safest and best place for you to stay is with me, at least for the time being. What do you think about it?"

I wouldn't have believed a goat could shrug, but Zook did.

"Works for me. And remember, I'm a boy."

I was torn between laughter and strangling the cute varmint. One glance at Logan told me he was leaning more toward the strangling idea.

The goat headed off. "I guess he's ready to go."

"Well, all right."I took Logan's offered hand.

As we passed by our picnic area, we grabbed the blanket, food containers, and garbage, then followed our new goat buddy out of the forest.

****

Zook trotted into Logan's rented apartment poked his furry head into each room, then back to us. "It'll do."

"I'm so glad."

The little goat looked up at Logan's six-plus feet. "There is no need for sarcasm."

We got Zook settled and spent a couple of hours helping Terri and Hunter.

Later that evening, Logan took me home. We stood on the porch of Terri's current home and I wondered just how amazing the kisses would be.

He took my hands in his. "Would you be interested in seeing that new science fiction movie at the Plaza?"

I narrowed my eyes. "Maybe."

"I was thinking maybe Wednesday night. I'll take

you to dinner first."

I gave up on teasing and answered him. "I'd really like that."

"Pick you up at seven?"

"I'll be waiting."

He kissed me then, and it was amazing.

I woke in the middle of the night wondering what in the world I was doing dating a bad boy type. Then I realized just how much my mom would hate that and returned to sleep with a little smile on my face.

****

I sat cross-legged on my borrowed bed, combing through information gathered on my laptop. The company Logan worked for looked pretty much like any other large corporation. There'd been a few complaints but nothing really bad. Until…

My breath caught, and I leaned closer to the screen.

"Lawsuit Filed Against New Century Research and Development Employees For Industrial Espionage," the headline read. The company's biggest rival filed the suit, and the article gave only a vague idea of what the two men and a woman had actually done. In fact, I wasn't sure what "industrial espionage" even really meant. I supposed it was time to do some research.

The noise from the backyard began as a low rumble but quickly built to a cacophony of voices, yelling, and then a high-pitched squeal. I muttered some seriously naughty words as I tore through the house.

The neighbor, Ms. Carlisle, was screaming at Zook. His head was poked through the fence and he was using her flower bed as a salad bar. He moved to a new spot as I headed that way, to access another section of the foliage. Suddenly he jumped back, snorted, shook his head like he'd been stung, and did a one-eighty turn to where he'd found some tasty pink flowers.

"Zook, get away from there!"

He looked at me for long enough to let me know he knew I was there, then turned back to the flowers. Meanwhile, Ms. Carlisle screamed.

I walked bravely over to the furry little pain in the ass. "Come on, Zook, you can't eat the nice lady's flowers.

Clearly, he didn't believe me. As I tried to move him away his hooves dug into the ground. Either he couldn't, or wouldn't, talk while other humans were around. Not that I seriously thought reasoning with him would get me anywhere. So I stayed as close to his head as I could so he couldn't easily kick me. Of course, there wasn't much I could do about his teeth or those sharp little horns on his head.

I gently put an arm around his back. "Zook, it's not nice to eat people's flowers."

He ignored me, so I tightened my grip.

"Come with me, and I'll find you something better to eat." Like maybe Logan.

"I'm calling the police!" Ms. Carlisle yelled. "I'm not living next to farm animals."

"We live next to a circus," I heard Terri mutter.

He finally let me pull him away and I led Zook into the house, wondering what to feed a wayward goat. "Do you like fresh veggies?"

"What do you think I was eating?"

I barely resisted the urge to roll my eyes. "Like carrots, celery, tomatoes."

"Yum."

I grabbed whatever I could find, put them on a paper plate, and set it on the floor in a corner.

"Thanks!" Zook wasted no time getting started on his dinner.

"You got some 'splaining to do, girl." Terri grabbed my sleeve and tugged.

In the living room, Hunter stood with arms crossed and did not look any happier than my best friend.

"He's a miniature goat, and his name is Zook."

"Where did he come from?" Hunter asked.

"He was in the woods. Logan and I found him there."

"So you're looking for the owner?"

"Not exactly."

"How do you know his name?"

I looked down at my t-shirt to make sure Terri hadn't set it on fire. "He told us."

"He what?" Hunter's eyes bulged, and I was a little worried about how red his neck had suddenly turned.

"He talks, but only to Logan and me."

"I thought you didn't like Logan." Terri smiled.

"He's not as bad as I thought, but what's that got to do with anything?"

"You two are soulmates, aren't you?" Terri's amused expression became more annoying.

"What the hell?" Hunter looked at us like we had both gone off the deep end.

"How could you possibly know that?" I said.

"You are!" Terri wiggled so hard she was almost bouncing.

Hunter asked before I could. "What makes you think they're soulmates?"

"You'd better start talking, girlfriend," I told her.

"Stephie's friend Madison and Gibson McFain have a dog named Gizmo. He can talk too, and nobody can hear him but the two of them."

"McFain is that documentary film dude, right?" I asked.

Terri nodded. "And Madison's soulmate."

"And their dog talks to them?"

"Yep, but only to them."

I tried to give her a scathing look, but I doubt I was very successful. "Why didn't you tell me?"

She shrugged. "It was just another weird Ugly Creek thing. How was I supposed to know you'd find yourself a furry romance detector?"

"I am much more than that," Zook said from the kitchen doorway.

"Yeah," I told him. "You're also a pain in the ass."

"He's talking to you, isn't he?" Terri moved closer to the goat. "I wish I could hear him."

"No, you don't."

Zook stuck his tongue out at me, and Terri giggled.

I turned back to the goat. "When did Logan bring you over here?"

"He didn't."

I stared at the critter in front of me. "So, how did you get here?"

"Magic."

I didn't beat my head against the wall, but it was a close call.

Beside me, Terri laughed, while Hunter rubbed his forehead.

Chapter 9

"Logan and I are going out to dinner and a movie tonight."

Terri grinned. "Of course you are." She patted my arm. "Have fun with your soulmate."

As she walked away, I considered the possibility that Logan and I really were soulmates. I'd never believed in the concept, feeling that one true love per person was statistically unreasonable. Of all the people in the world, what were the chances of two who were meant to be together actually meeting and figuring out they were destined to be together?

In fact, I wasn't even sure I liked Logan, much less loved him. Were we supposed to take the word of a goat? How the hell was that even a question? To distract me from confusion that was giving me a headache, I called the B&B for an update. The good news was they were finished repairing the fire damage. Followed, of course, by the bad news: there were still a lot of little details that needed to be taken care of before they could open for guests again.

So, for now, I was stuck bunking with my best friend and her man. Not that I really minded, but a bit of privacy would be nice. I sighed and headed off to figure out what to wear on my big date.

I sincerely hoped Zook didn't think he needed to chaperone or something.

****

By the time Logan picked me up, my host couple had gone off to work on their house, so at least I didn't have to deal with Terri's teasing. I will admit to being nervous. Yes, Logan and I had been hanging out together and had even been sent a goat by the powers that do crazy stuff, or whatever. Still, I barely knew Logan, couldn't read him and wasn't sure I trusted him. Though, admittedly, he'd been nothing but nice to me.

He knocked, and I jumped just a little. Laughing at myself, I opened the front door and motioned him inside the house.

"You look adorable," he said.

"Thank you." My face heated as I glanced down at the soft green blouse and black pants I'd chosen to wear.

His fingers touched my cheek, and he grinned. "You're even cuter when you're embarrassed."

"You just like to annoy me, don't you?"

He grinned even wider. "It's so easy."

I rolled my eyes. "How's the furry menace? Is he still mad he had to go back to your place?"

Logan groaned. "He thinks he's king, and I'm his servant."

I couldn't stop myself. I started laughing.

Logan, though, gave me the evil eye. "He wanted to come on our date."

I tried to stifle any more levity, but I was still smiling when he put his arm around me and all but shoved me out the door.

We drove to a mall near Knoxville, had pizza at a small restaurant and were at the theatre complex in plenty of time. Logan paid for everything, and since I tended to change jobs fairly frequently, I was happy not to dig into what money I had. And after all, Logan flaunted his high-paying position with a big company.

We headed into the huge theater with the floor that sloped toward the screen. Red carpet, heavy red curtains along the sides and covering the screen, red upholstered seats, the smell of fresh, hot popcorn permeated the whole building. I sighed happily. Movie theaters always made me feel good.

"So, should we sit in the back row and neck like teenagers?"

How about we sit in the middle and actually watch the film."

"Party pooper."

He stuck his bottom lip out and gave me a big-eyed puppy look that had me shaking with laughter. I was trying hard to keep to a reasonable level.

We found a middle seat to one side and yeah, we did get in some kissing and such too. At least until one scene had me grabbing Logan and hanging on for dear life.

I expected the movie to be more slasher or horror than true science fiction. What I didn't count on was the film quickly becoming a creepy, chill-producing story that left me shaky and vaguely paranoid.

I was grateful for Logan's arm around me as he walked me out to his car. He stood by as I got in, then went around and slid into the driver's side. I thought I was steady by then, but when he closed his door, I jumped and squealed like a little girl.

He put a hand on my shoulder and studied me with narrowed eyes and a scrunched forehead.

"Are you all right?"

I looked down to keep him from seeing the color of my suddenly hot face. "I'm fine."

"Are you going to tell me what's wrong, or am I going to have to guess?"

I smiled but didn't meet his gaze. "You think you can, huh?"

He leaned so close his lips touched my ear. "That movie seemed kinda creepy to me too."

I saw no sign of teasing, only a quiet warmth. "I'm not usually a wuss.

"I get that. But when something gets to you, it can be hard to shake it off." He took my hands in his. "Why don't I take you home with me? I'll protect you from that horrible movie monster."

I gave him a long, speculative look. "Okay, but who will protect you?"

"I'm not scared of a fictional boogeyman." He made a point of looking to the left, the right, in the mirrors, over my shoulder.

I bit my lip to hold back the smile. "Think we're safe?"

"Probably."

"You're not right in the head, Montgomery."

"Never said I was, babe."

"Don't call me babe."

"Sorry." He grinned.

He wasn't, but I ignored him.

****

"Well, it's about time you two got home."

I screamed a little, and Logan moved so he was between me and the source of the voice. Zook stood in front of us. Something so furry and adorable really shouldn't be able to glare like that, but he was managing it just fine.

"You scared the socks off, Dia."

I didn't bother to point out how Logan had a steel grip on my hand, and I could feel the tremor in his body.

"I need food, water, and to go outside," our precious little pain in the butt insisted.

We looked at each other, groaned, then did what he asked.

A few minutes later, he promptly curled up on an old blanket in the corner and went to sleep. It was close to midnight when Logan and I finally carried glasses of wine to the couch. He slid an arm around my shoulders, and I leaned against him. We sipped silently for a few minutes, and the stress of the last few weeks drained away. I just wanted to sit there forever and enjoy the feel of the strong, masculine body beside me.

"Tired?"

"A little."

"I'll take it slow then." He leaned in and pressed his lips over mine.

I reached my non-wine-holding arm up to touch his face and hair. My body arched a bit in an attempt to close the distance between us. The feel of the glass in my hand pressing against my body pulled me back to reality.

"The wine."

Logan moved back enough to take my glass, then sat both glasses on the coffee table. When he turned back, his eyes had gone almost black, and my heart beat against my chest like it was trying to get out.

He leaned in, sliding his arm around my shoulders, and once again covered my mouth with his. He drove me crazy with his kisses. His tongue teased mine. Then he moved his mouth to tease my cheeks, my ear, my throat. While he scattered kisses and tiny licks all over my face and neck, he edged his fingers down to the hem of my shirt, slipped underneath, then moved up the side of my breast. He touched my nipple, and I gasped. His deep chuckle sent tingles up my spine.

He spent some time using his fingers to tease my nipples while his mouth made its way down to take over. Then while his mouth licked, kissed, and sucked at my nipples, his freed hands slid down my back to my behind. He edged me toward him, and I reached around to hold him closer.

"If you want to stop, you'd better let me know," His voice was tight and rough.

Since actions speak louder than words, I tightened my arms around him and used the leverage to slide my leg across him to straddle his lap. I moved slowly, deliberately, until the bulge in his pants rubbed against the most sensitive part of my own body.

"You're killing me." He moaned.

"Can't have that." I gasped. Feeling the intensity of incredible arousal myself, I decided we needed to move things along.

Seeming to arrive at the same conclusion, he stood and peeled the clothes off me slowly. Not one to patiently wait my turn, I put my hands to work, removing his clothes from one amazing male body. Which, I quickly discovered, was hard and mouth-watering.

"Bedroom." His voice was deep and sexy.

Naked, we moved to the bed as one. We lay on our sides facing each other, and he immediately returned to using his mouth and hands to drive me insane. Naturally, I used my own hands to explore his neck, and shoulders, and back, and…oh my goodness, what a tight ass!

He groaned and shoved me onto my back. Using his knees, he edged my legs apart, then reached between them. I'm pretty sure I levitated. He chuckled as he quickly rolled on a condom that he'd apparently conjured from thin air. In no hurry, he went back to using his mouth to drive me out of my mind while he used his fingers to stoke my body from hot to flame.

And then he was inside me. I moaned like I'd never moaned before, as he slowly built up speed. It was both a tiny fraction of a second and all of eternity until together we reached a place I never dreamed existed.

A world that belonged to the two of us alone.

When we returned to earth, he pulled the covers over us, snuggled me against him, and we slept.

Chapter 10

The sun peeked between the curtains when I woke from a strange dream of arguing with a man I'd never met for some reason I didn't understand. The realization that I was in Logan's apartment and snuggled next to him was rapidly followed by a strong need to pee.

I rushed to the bathroom then tiptoed back. Logan had rolled from his side to his back. The slice of sun from between the curtains lit his face and upper body. I perched on the side and watched him sleep. His dark eyelashes lay above the sharp bones of his cheeks. His wide, firm mouth was just slightly open as if inviting me to kiss him awake.

Instead, I continued my inspection. His shoulders were broad, his chest slowly narrowing to his waist. The sheet covered him from there down, but I could see the outline of his firm thighs and his man parts. I was almost drooling as I ran my fingers over one shoulder.

The vision hit me so hard I almost tumbled off the bed.

Logan was with a group of people, all in lab coats.

"We have to find this Bigfoot creature." Dr. Lynch pounded a fist on the table in front of him.

"They're certainly valuable," someone agreed.

"They could make us rich," another voice pointed out. "Figuring out how they're different from humans is a big deal."

"Just proving their existence could mean millions."

"Possible ancestor of humanity," Logan said. *"More valuable than anything else on earth."*

I stared down at Logan, only seeing a shadow of him behind the vision. I was accustomed to having visions, but this was like nothing I'd ever experienced before. What the hell was going on?

"Dia."

I fought away the tendrils of the vision, and the room swirled into focus.

"Are you all right?" He sat up and reached for me.

Before I even thought about what I was doing, I jumped up and backed away. "Who are you?"

An expression of utter shock filled his face. "Honey, it's me. It's Logan."

"I know your name." I took another step backwards, reaching down to grab my pants as I went. "You want to use the Bigfoot. You don't care if they get hurt. What kind of a monster are you?"

He slid out of bed and gaped at me as if I were the monster. "How can you think something like that after what we just shared?"

"I saw a vision." I yanked my pants on without bothering to search for my panties. My bra hung over a lamp, and I pulled it around me, somehow managing to twist the damn thing, but I ignored the discomfort.

"I saw you and your coworkers. I heard what you were talking about."

"Wait, no, it's not like that."

By this time, I'd retrieved my top from where one of us had tossed it under a chair and pulled it on. I was putting on my sandals when I realized Logan stood in front of me. He was stark naked and without a doubt, the most beautiful man I'd ever seen. I sucked in my breath and almost tripped over my shoes.

"Sit down, and we can talk this out. Please."

I met his gaze then. His gorgeous dark eyes were filled with hurt and confusion. My heart tore.

"I have to leave."

"Let me explain."

I reached up to touch my fingers to his lips but caught myself at the last moment. "Nothing like that has ever happened to me before, and I need time to figure things out."

He nodded slowly. "Just don't write us off before I get a chance to tell you my side of whatever you think you know."

My back straightened, and my chin kicked up. "I don't think, damn it. I know!" I spun and stomped out of his apartment, grabbing my panties on the way. I stuffed the underwear in my purse and headed for my car.

Why did people keep doubting my ability? Was I that scary? Tears filled my eyes as I pulled away from the curb. Damn, sometimes I hated my so-called gift.

I took my time getting back to Terri's house, and when I arrived, I considered not going in at all. There was another car in the driveway, a silver mid-size that I recognized as my sister's. It was only the fact that I had nowhere else to go that convinced me to walk up the driveway and climb the steps.

I'd barely put my foot on the porch when the door swung open to Finley glaring hard at me. If it wasn't for Terri standing with a reassuring smile behind her, I might have turned around and gone the other way.

I shoved past my sister and walked into the living room.

"Scott broke up with me," Finley said. "I hope you're happy."

"I'm not happy he hurt you, but I am glad you two aren't getting married."

"Meanwhile, you're out having a good time." She used her thumb and index finger to gingerly pull my panties from my purse. "Were you with Scott?"

What a disgusting thought. "No! Scott's a cheating jerk."

"So you say."

"So I know."

"You just can't stand for me to be happy. You've always envied me."

I stared at my sister. Long inky-black hair, size three figure, taller than me by almost six inches. Guys tripped when she walked by. The only thing I had on her was my success in school. She did okay, but I just plain loved learning.

"I'm not jealous, and I do want you to be happy. I knew you weren't likely to believe me, but I told you about Scott anyway because I couldn't stand for him to treat you like that."

"Like what?" Finley's eyes blazed with anger. "He treats me like a princess. He gives me little gifts. He's there for me when I need him."

I took a long, slow breath and looked her dead in the eyes. "He's cheating on you."

"You're crazy."

"You're my sister. You know me. I've had the ability to see and know things my whole life. How can you dismiss everything you've witnessed over the years?"

"Because it's all bull, that's why. You can't possibly do the things you claim you can do. It's all a trick, and Mom knows how you do it."

I'd held on to my temper as long as I could. "It's not a trick. And yes, I think Mom does know how I do it, but she refuses to believe what she sees with her own two eyes."

Finley rolled her eyes. "You just like being a weirdo."

This was getting us nowhere, and I knew from experience my sister could go on and on for hours. I groaned and struggled to think of something that might shut her up.

"That's not a very nice thing to say to your sister." Terri stepped toward Finley and glared at her.

Finley crossed her arms and glared back. "She's telling lies about my fiancé."

I blurted, "I thought the two of you broke up." Yeah, it was a dumb thing to say, but my nerves were dancing on each other.

Finley looked at me with an expression of sheer fury. "He got tired of your crazy accusations."

I wanted badly to scream at her, but that wouldn't help. I couldn't just stand there and let her get more worked up. When she looked away for a moment, I caught Terri's gaze and focused on barely moving my mouth as I whispered so quietly. Finley wouldn't have heard it if she'd been standing right beside us, "I have to get out of here."

Terri lowered her chin in the smallest hint of a nod. "Finley, I know you've seen Dia do her thing, she's always told us what she sees, so we know what's going on. You know, I'd bet my next advance check you've never known her to be wrong."

"She's wrong now."

"That's still to be determined." Terri slid over to me and took my hand. Immediately I got a clear image of a park. I saw picnic tables, areas for playing football and such, even a sign that told me this was Bigfoot Park, and it was on the north side of town. I looked at her, and she winked.

"Let's sit down and have some tea." Terri let go of me, put an arm around Finley, and shoved my unruly sister toward the kitchen.

I started toward them, moving slowly and watching for my opportunity. When they turned the corner into the kitchen, I took the opportunity to slip out the door quietly. There was only so much a girl could take, and this girl was done. I jumped into my tiny car and headed to safer places.

****

Twenty minutes later, I sat cross-legged on a picnic table at Bigfoot Park. It was midmorning on a school day, so there wasn't a crowd. A handful of small children played hard, and a couple of beleaguered mothers watched from a nearby bench.

The kids climbed, ran, and squealed; the grownups talked, and I sat staring off into space. I'd come to Ugly Creek for some quiet and a chance to let go of the hole my family's attitude tore in me. Just because they didn't believe in psychic ability did not mean they had to be so nasty to me. I was tired of being treated like I belonged in one of those creepy old asylums like you see in horror movies.

Worse, I hated that I had a hard time shaking the

blow to my confidence their attitude caused. It had turned into a lifelong struggle, this need to believe in myself and have faith that I could actually have dreams and see them fulfilled.

Abruptly, Logan's face filled my head, bringing with it the warm fuzzy feeling when he said he believed I could read minds, even though I couldn't read his. He'd accepted my gift without proof. My own flesh and blood refused to believe what I see, even with an abundance of proof.

I was trying to wrap my brain around the knowledge when footsteps came toward me. For just a second, my heart hoped it was Logan, but I knew before I turned that it wasn't.

"Can I throw your sister off Clingmans Dome?"

"Isn't that way up in the mountains?"

Terri grinned. "The highest point in Tennessee."

I considered the idea. "You know, it seems that Tennessee might just be my new home. So, I want to learn about scenic spots. Especially the good places for unloading problems."

She laughed but then took on a more serious expression. "New home, huh?"

I shrugged. "This little town is growing on me. I'm thinking moving here, close to people who actually care about me, might not be a bad idea."

"I'm glad you like it here." I didn't have to touch her. I could feel the happiness radiating from her.

She used one foot to shove herself up, so she was sitting beside me on the wooden table. Storm clouds seemed to be gathering around her face, and I braced myself.

"Now, what did Logan do to you?"

Pain filled my heart, weighing it down until I was afraid it would slide right out of my belly. "It's complicated."

"Dia, I've known you since kindergarten, and I've never seen you this upset." She gave me a one-armed hug that almost broke a rib. "Now spill, I need details to plan the getting-even party."

I started to tell her I really couldn't talk about it, but if I tried that, she'd torture me for details. Besides, I knew I needed to get it out. So I forced myself to speak. "Apparently, I *can* read Logan."

"What? Wait, you said you weren't getting anything,"

"I wasn't."

"So, did something change?" Her eyes widened. "Was it because—"

"I can read him when he's asleep," I spoke quickly before she followed that thought all the way through.

"Asleep?" Was that a hint of disappointment in her voice?

"Yes. This morning I woke up, and Logan was still asleep. I touched his arm, and I saw…" I covered my face with my hands and wished I could forget what I saw.

"What did you see?" Her hand gently rubbed my back and shoulders. "Just spit it out, girlfriend. You'll feel better."

"I saw him with his boss and a couple of his coworkers. They were talking about doing research." I worked at catching my breath again.

"What kind of research?"

"Bigfoot," I forced out.

"The big furry critters?"

"Yes."

"Maybe they were talking about anthropological research. Observation. Learning their language."

"No. They were talking about…" I closed my eyes and tears slid down my cheeks. "The differences between Bigfoot and humans."

"But maybe…"

I shook my head. "They want money. They think they can leverage the physiological differences for who knows what kinds of research. Logan's boss said just proving their existence would make them millions."

"Maybe Logan won't go along with them."

I shook my head. "He was right there with the rest."

"Maybe there's an explanation."

"He told me right out how important money is to him. He knows he could get a job doing good things, but he makes more working for New Century Research and Development."

"I knew there was something about him that bugged me, but I never even considered anything like this."

"Me either."

She wiggled for a bit, then looked at me. "You know, even though both of us have doubts about the company, neither of us feel he's the kind of person who could be involved with something harmful to the Bigfoot tribe. Plus, Hunter's been friends with Logan for a long time, and he's not that bad a judge of character."

Tears welled up in my throat. "But I know what I saw."

"Okay, but maybe he had to go along with the rest.

He might have been afraid of getting fired on the spot. Doesn't mean if it comes right down to actually doing anything detrimental, he wouldn't back out."

"We can't ignore this, though."

"I agree." She hopped off the table. "Come on."

"Where are we going?" I asked as I followed her lead.

"Antiquing."

I was totally confused until my brain kicked in. "Stephie can contact the Bigfoot tribe?"

Terri shrugged. "Don't know, but I'm pretty sure Jake can."

We got in my tiny car and headed toward town.

"You know," Terri said. "I told Finley I had to run to the store. She'll be expecting me back soon."

"She'll be okay."

"If she breaks my arms, you'll have to type for me."

"If she hurts you, she'll need somebody to feed her."

Terri stared wide-eyed for a minute, then grinned.

****

"You're sure about this?"

"Positive." I looked into Jake's eyes, willing him to see the truth in mine.

We were at Blackwood Antiques, where we'd been for over an hour. Stephie was working with customers. Jake, Terri, and I sat in Jake's office at the back of the store.

"I just can't believe Logan would be involved in something like that." Jake shook his head. "He's such a straight shooter."

"Look, I know it sounds crazy, but I've had these

visions my entire life, as did my maternal grandmother." I was getting wound up to present a logical argument regarding psychic visions and how they've been part of my life as far back as I could remember when I realized he was chuckling quietly. I thought sure he was laughing at me. My hands balled into fists and I sucked in a hard breath.

He held his hands up in surrender. "I'm just thinking how I live in a town with Bigfoot, aliens, fairies, shapeshifters, and who knows what else. You being psychic is one of the least weird things around here. I believe you saw what you saw."

"So you'll warn the Bigfoot?"

"Of course I will. I would never take a chance like that." He smiled. "I wouldn't be surprised, though, if they aren't already one step ahead of us."

Well, that threw me for a loop. "Why would you think that?"

"Because they always are." He picked up his cell phone off the desk. "Now, if you ladies will excuse me, I need to make some calls."

We said our goodbyes and went back to the store proper. Stephie was herding cats…I mean customers, so we waved toward her and headed toward the exit.

We were almost there when the shop door flew open, and Finley marched in. She stopped two feet in front of us.

"Hello, Terri. So your desperate need to get food for dinner involved picking up a few antiques? And you ran into my errant sister. How convenient."

I managed to resist the urge to deck her. "Okay, Finley, you made your point. This is between the two of us. Leave Terri out of it."

"Fine with me."

I held out my keys toward my friend. "Here, go home. You don't need to be part of this."

Terri crossed her arms. "No way. I'm not leaving you alone with her."

Finley's face went bright reddish-purple. "I'm her sister."

"Well," Terri glared at her. "Right now, you're acting more like a spoiled brat."

"Excuse me?"

"'Dia's trying to protect you, and all you've done is bitch at her."

"How is this even any of your business?"

Terri got so close to Finley that I could barely see the light between them. "Because she is my best friend. I've known her most of our lives, and she's always there for me when I need her."

"She only does what benefits her."

"Like moving to an apartment close to your office?"

Finley's gaze caught mine, and the heat of her glare could have caused a fire. "Oh, so having a nice apartment doesn't appeal to you? Would you rather be back in that overgrown closet that you lived in before? Besides, you only stay employed for a few weeks at a time anyway. It really doesn't matter where you live."

My face went molten. "That's not true. I've been at Kathy's bakery for almost a year."

"Yep, the longest you've ever had a job. Not to mention, you likely don't have it now since you took off."

"I made arrangements."

Finley raised one eyebrow. "Dia, I went to school

with Kathy. We still have lunch from time to time."

I gave up, dropping my chin and raising my hands in surrender. "Okay, fine. I probably lost that one too. It's hard when you know things you don't want to know."

Stephie appeared and put a hand on my shoulder and the other on Finley. In a low voice, she asked, "Hey, guys. What's with the free-for-all?"

Guilt spread hot and fast through my veins. "I'm sorry, Stephie."

"Would you be interested in some antique dresses?" She kept one hand on my sister's shoulder as she pointed to a display on the other side of the store. Moments later, she and Finley moved toward the clothing.

Terri and I ducked out the door. "Where is that Clingmans Dome?"

"It's on the Tennessee-North Carolina line up in the national park. Not far from Gatlinburg."

"Nice drive."

Terri nodded. "Sure is. Maybe we should check it out one day. Do you think maybe Finley might like to go with us?"

"We might have to convince her a little." I smiled, but as I did, an emptiness settled in my middle.

When we arrived at my tiny car, Terri hesitated. "You okay?"

"She's my sister. How can she not even know me?" Tears filled my eyes, and I blinked hard to force them back.

"How about I drive?"

It would definitely be safer. I nodded, and we climbed in.

"It's okay to be upset, Dia."

"I hate when she gets to me. "

"You got hit hard twice back to back by people close to you. People you should be able to trust." She turned onto an unpaved back road, went down it a way, pulled over onto a wide area, and turned to me. "Let it out, my friend. You tend to hold things in, and I'm afraid you'll have a heart attack or something."

"I'm okay."

She rolled her eyes, the rat. "One, your sister's driving you crazy. Two, you're sure Logan and his work buddies are planning something that could harm the Bigfoot tribe."

My confidence vanished in a puff of reality. "In my vision I heard them talking about it."

"And you're positive Logan wasn't just trying to save his job?"

Tears ran down my face, and I grabbed a tissue from the little box I kept in my car. "It sure didn't seem like that. He said they could be the ancestors of humans and more valuable than anything on earth."

"Maybe he was trying to convince the others not to hurt the Bigfoot."

"I want to believe that. More than anything, I want to believe he couldn't do something so heinous."

Terri gently squeezed my arm. "I thought so."

"Thought what?"

"That you're in love with him."

I started to deny it, to shove the whole emotional mess way down inside me. But I couldn't do it. I gazed into my best friend's eyes. "What am I going to do?"

"You're going to find out what's really going on with your rakish boyfriend."

My heart twisted. "My visions have never been wrong."

She shook her head. "I'm not saying they're wrong, just that you're taking one little section of a conversation out of context. You don't know all the facts yet."

"I want to believe there's a mistake, but I just got through arguing with my sister that she has to believe what I saw. That's pretty hypocritical of me."

"What did you see your sister's worthless fiancé do?"

My face went hot. "He and Lena were making out, and clothes were coming off."

"That's totally different than hearing a bit of conversation. There's no uncertainty about what was going on."

I closed my eyes and leaned my head back against the seat. "I am so confused."

"You need to cry."

I groaned. "No, I don't."

She put an arm around me and pulled me against her shoulder. "Yes, my friend, you do."

I continued to fight for a moment, then gave up and let the tears win. I felt her warm hand against my shoulder as I allowed the stress and worry to wash away.

A few minutes later, I sat up and wiped my face. "I'm a mess."

"But you feel better, right?"

"Yes."

"Good. We'll go home and have cookies before I have to make dinner."

I studied her as we pulled out onto the main road.

"How do you do it?"

"Do what?"

"Always know what humans need? You're not completely human, yet you're better at knowing what we need than we are."

"Not better." She shot me a grin. "I just notice more."

"Still, it's pretty amazing." I sniffed and wiped at my face with a tissue.

"Dogs pay a lot of attention to human emotion, Dia. We love to make humans happy. Then we can bask in the good feeling for hours, days if we're lucky."

I bit back the grin. "So, making me cry made you happy?"

"No. The relief you felt after you cried made me happy."

"Thank you."

She tilted her head in acknowledgment, "You're very welcome."

I leaned back and focused on calming down. When I felt a little braver, I took a quick look in the mirror behind the sun visor and groaned. My eyes were red, and mascara was smeared under the red. I grabbed tissues and set to work making myself look decent.

I was working at reclaiming my face when Terri let out a big sigh. "In all honesty, I have a hard time understanding how pure humans deal with stuff. You can't shift forms and run like crazy until you're exhausted and then sleep." She shrugged. "That always makes me feel better."

"You know humans do run to deal with emotional stuff too."

"But only a handful of them. For a dog, it's like

111

crying for humans. We need it."

"You can do either."

She nodded. "But running's the best. Crying helps, but running clears my head more."

Hmm, maybe I'd consider going for a run. Or not. I was strangely wrung out. Maybe from not sleeping much last night. Damn that man!

Terri pulled her car into the driveway, and Hunter stood in the yard, near the fence line, glaring down at one annoying goat.

"Oh, good grief!" I muttered as I climbed out and headed toward my little problem goat. "What's he been into now?"

"The neighbor's flowers. Again."

"Oh, Zook!" I glared, but he just kept innocently chewing on grass.

Hunter sighed. "I drag him out of the flowers and put him over here where he can munch grass in peace, but as soon as I turn my back, he's into Miss C's precious flowers again." He shot a glance toward the neighboring house. "She scares me."

"She scares us all," Terri said from behind me.

As she passed by, she squeezed my shoulder, then grabbed Hunter with both hands. He wrapped his arms around her waist, lifted her off the ground, and proceeded to kiss her. Then he picked her up and carried her inside.

I turned back to the grass-chomping annoyance. "Why do you keep eating Mrs. Carlisle's flowers?"

"They're yummy."

"You can't just eat something because it tastes good. Those flowers don't belong to you."

"Did I mention how yummy they are?"

"Stay out of the flowers."

"I'll think about it."

I turned toward the house, knowing I'd have to keep a close eye on Zook.

"Some of Crazy Woman's flowers smell funny." He looked at me without the usual aloof expression.

"What are you saying?" I asked.

"There's something in that flower bed that shouldn't be there. Something that smells really bad."

I considered what he'd said as I walked into the house. Terri had mentioned her dad—also a were-dog—said something similar. Something was wrong, and I wasn't crazy about my best friend living next door.

A peek out the window told me Zook was still eating grass and behaving—for the moment, anyway. I set my phone to remind me to check again in fifteen minutes.

Just then, a silver car pulled off the road. I groaned out loud. I thought about running and hiding, but she'd just find me. I opened the front door.

"Hi, Finley."

"Bite me," she replied as she headed straight toward me.

I crossed my arms and waited for her. "Is this a continuation, or did I do something new?"

"Wasn't breaking my heart enough?"

"I was trying to protect you, but do go on."

"I'm going back home to try and make things right with Scott."

I closed my eyes and let the sigh slide through my body.

"Why don't you want me to be happy?"

Tears stung my eyes. "I do want you to be happy. Don't you understand? I'm trying to keep you from getting your heart broken."

She studied me for a moment. "Do you really believe Scott's cheating?"

I swallowed the need to scream. "I saw it in my vision. One of those visions I've had all my life."

"Like when you knew there was a fire at the school?"

"Yes."

"Or when Aunt Margaret broke her leg?"

"Or the hundreds of other visions I've had."

She groaned. "I just can't believe Scott would cheat on me."

"I understand, really I do. But I see what I see. I have no control over the visions." I touched her arm. "And they've never been wrong."

Finley dropped her head, allowing her long hair to cover her face. After a minute, she looked at me again while pulling her hair back with her fingers. "I'm still going home to try to work things out."

My heart dropped to my knees. "Just be careful."

She surprised me with a quick hug before she headed for her car. She was almost there when she stopped, looked over her shoulder, and said, "I will." Then she got in her car and headed down the road.

I sent out a silent prayer of hope before I headed in to help with lunch.

****

Four hours later, I struggled to keep a huge sheet of drywall against the wooden frame of a wall in the master bedroom of Terri and Hunter's renovation. Hunter used an electric screwdriver to hang the drywall, and he was pretty adept at doing it. Still, the huge sheet was heavy and awkward, and I wasn't the tallest or strongest woman in the world. Terri and I had been working together until she'd had to get some supplies. It hadn't been bad to start with, but it didn't take long for my body to start complaining.

Hunter finished the current sheet and lifted the next to line it up. "Just a couple more, and we'll be finished."

I forced a weak smile and moved to hold the giant rectangle against the frame where the wall would be. It was a struggle, but I hung on, using my strength and body weight to keep the piece against the studs. There were footsteps, but my focus was on not letting the drywall move.

I knew who was there before the big, male body pressed against my back. Long arms reached past me and up, and the weight of the drywall was all but gone.

"Better?" Logan's breath brushed my ear.

"I had it under control."

"No doubt in my mind."

I couldn't figure out whether the tone was sarcastic or not, so I just ignored him. A couple more minutes, and Hunter was finished. When both men stepped back, I followed suit, allowing myself a long, thankful sigh.

"Hello, Dia."

"Logan." I glanced at him, then away. His shoulders slumped, and his eyes were red.

Hunter grabbed another sheet of drywall and easily moved it to the next section Logan moved to help without his usual energy. I clearly wasn't needed, so I decided to see if there was something I could get into. Pain, loss, maybe regret. Whatever he was feeling, I was in no mood to discuss it. I heard Terri coming in, so I rushed off to see if she could use my help.

Turns out she wanted to work on installing the tile in the master bath and was happy to make use of my unskilled labor. It took a little time and a couple of do-overs for us to get the hang of the job. After that, we discovered we worked well together. It wasn't long before the classic white subway tile was installed.

Terri's smile was big, happy, and self-satisfied. "Well, I guess we showed the men."

"It does look really nice."

She tiptoed down the hall a little way, then motioned for me to follow her to the kitchen. "We deserve a treat." She pulled a package of chocolate chip cookies from behind a box of cabinet hardware. "I hid them so the boys wouldn't eat without us."

We sat on the floor, munched, and relaxed. I enjoyed the cookies and conversation, but my mind kept flipping back to the vision I'd had and the man I couldn't seem to stop obsessing over.

****

A few minutes later, Terri and Hunter were trying to decide how to arrange the kitchen. I stepped outside to check on Zook and get some fresh air.

The goat was calmly chewing on wild flowers. I rolled my neck and stretched the tight muscles. Between the stress of the morning and the hard physical work, I was stiff, sore, and drained. I was strolling around the side of the house when a familiar voice drifted my way. I knew I should turn around and leave well enough alone, but I just couldn't make my feet go there. Instead, I headed toward the back of the house.

Logan's back was turned, and he paced while he talked to someone on his phone. "Of course I will. I'm not backing out now. I'll do what has to be done."

He turned then, and his gaze met mine. "Gotta go," he said and clicked off his phone. "Dia."

"Logan."

"How are you?" Was that concern in his face?

"I'm fine," I said, hoping he wouldn't realize it was a lie. "How are you?

"You had a vision while I was asleep, didn't you?"

"Yes," I admitted.

"And it was so bad you went running out of there like the place was on fire. Wanna tell me what you think you saw?"

I shoved my trembling hands into the pockets of my jeans and decided there wasn't anything to lose at this point. "I saw you, your boss, and a couple of your coworkers talking about your current project. Your real current project."

He moved toward me so quickly I actually gasped. "Things aren't always what they seem."

I let my frustration and irritation show. "It seemed pretty clear to me. You're willing to hurt—"

His lips covered mine, kept me from saying what I wanted. I pushed at him, but he kept on with the amazing kisses until I wrapped my arms around him and gave in to the enjoyment. His kisses moved down my neck and up to my ear.

"There are things I can't tell you right now," he whispered.

My breath sucked in hard. "What!"

"Shhh," He nuzzled my neck again. "I'm being monitored."

I almost laughed. "You're a spy?"

He kissed my lips so hard it hurt a little. He pulled

away and nuzzled the other side of my neck. "I can't explain right now. Just please don't give up on me."

"I don't want to," I whispered.

"Don't say anything to anybody, not even Terri or Hunter. Please give me some time."

I nodded, wondering if I wasn't making a major mistake. I should trust my visions, not my heart.

"I love you," he whispered, then walked away.

I remained, frozen in place. Logan scratched Zook's head before he got into his yellow car. He looked my way for long enough for me to feel his pain and longing before he backed out onto the road and drove away.

I lingered for a long time, just staring into the direction Logan had gone. What should I make of this development?

Was he being truthful, or just covering his tight, sexy ass?

Chapter 11

I heard nothing from Logan for two long days. I tried hard to pretend that didn't bother me, but not seeing him drove me nuts. Finally, I decided I couldn't take the questions and uncertainty anymore. I drove into town and past the building where he worked. His car wasn't there. Was something wrong? Was he sick? Had he left Ugly Creek?

It finally dawned on me that his wasn't the only car not in the lot. There were maybe a third of the usual number. It'd started back toward Terri's when I remembered my vision. I didn't want to believe what I'd seen, but checking things out wouldn't hurt. Right?

About ten minutes later, I drove down the back road that dipped into the forest. There were several vehicles parked in a small cleared area, including one brightly colored yellow sports car.

I slowed down but didn't stop. I told myself I'd found out what I wanted to know, that he was alive, still in Ugly Creek, and at work. Now the best thing to do was to go back to Terri's and mind my own business. If he was a part of a plan that could hurt the creatures, there was nothing I could do. Same if he was involved in some kind of spy thing. If that was the case, When Logan wanted to tell me more, he would.

I kept going in the opposite direction to Ugly Creek, deeper and deeper into the forest area. I had to turn around. Driving nowhere was ridiculous. So, I turned around.

I was almost back to where I'd seen Logan's car, when I saw a wide place and pulled far enough in that my tiny car wouldn't be obvious from the road. I tried really hard to convince myself to go home. I needed to get out of there now, I told myself. Then I locked the car and started walking.

I knew being there was A Bad Idea. If Logan was lying, confronting him out in the middle of nowhere was not smart. Then again, if he told me the truth, I could be screwing all manner of things up. I might even endanger Logan's life—or my own, though either premise seemed pretty dang farfetched.

There was a clear trail across the road from the parked cars, and I headed that way. At first, I went at a good clip, not really worried about being seen. Lots of people walked in the woods, and I was on public property. Then, as I got further in, the vegetation blocked the sunlight, and the world looked darker with every step. My stomach twisted, and I had a strong urge to turn and run in the other direction. Logan was a big boy. He didn't need—or want—my help. I should go back to Terri's and let the boys play. Whatever he was doing wasn't my business.

The sound of voices caught my attention. Whoever was having this conversation was far enough away that they weren't understandable from where I stood. I strolled closer, listening hard to try to pick out words or the sound of a familiar voice. Though anxious to find out what was really going on, I forced myself to move slowly, carefully.

As I got closer, I saw the corner of a small, metal

building. The sound of a small air conditioner whined from the other side of the building. The voices were closer and sounded like they were coming from outside.

"It's an amazing opportunity, and we'd be idiots not to take advantage of it."

Miles Lynch, Logan's boss. I fought back the disgust that twisted my gut and moved a little closer. He stood near a door into the metal building. He held a cigarette, which I guess was the reason he was outside.

"Those creatures are sentient." Logan.

I moved closer, using a huge tree for cover.

"So?" Lynch's voice was cold metal, and I wanted to throw up. "You've never been squeamish before."

"I don't want to go to jail."

"Don't worry about that. I spoke with the company lawyer, and he said there shouldn't be any problems. Besides, we'll be out of this backward little town before anybody realizes what's happening."

"True." Logan was leaning against the building and not smoking.

He shifted his position, and I caught a glimpse of his expression that made me believe he was telling the truth about going along but not believing in what the company was doing.

"Now to catch one of the creatures," Lynch said.

"They must be very intelligent," Logan said. "It's possible we may not be able to catch one."

Lynch laughed again, and I cringed. "They're animals, and we're humans. We'll get them, one way or the other. "

Okay, that was quite enough. Swallowing hard to hold my growing nausea at bay, I stepped back. I shouldn't have come. I should have done what Logan asked and let him handle whatever it was he was tangled up in.

A hand gripped my upper arm so hard, I thought a bear grabbed me. Then I saw the real culprit. He was not much taller than me, but he made up for it by being broad. Seriously, the guy looked like a rectangle with a tiny head.

"What do you think you're doing?"

"Leaning against a tree." I tried to pull my arm loose, but he only tightened his grip. Meanwhile, visions I did not want to see flashed through my mind.

This guy was a serious creep.

"You're spying on us, aren't you?"

"I don't know who the hell you even are." I yanked my arm again, knowing he'd just make it hurt worse. The dirtbag's life was a litany of petty crime, misogyny, and narcissistic fantasy.

"Come with me." He dragged me with him toward the front of the building, where Logan and Lynch stood.

Logan gasped. I tried to give him a little smile, but my captor twisted my arm again.

"Well, well, what have we here?" Lynch came over to me.

"She was spying on us," the ugly square-shaped man said.

"I was hiking, got tired, and leaned against a tree." I glared hard at the boss.

"And it's a coincidence that you stopped right here?"

"I heard voices, and I was curious."

"Logan, you need to keep better control over your girlfriend."

"She's not my girlfriend."

I was pretty sure he had a reason for what he said, but it hurt just the same. So I aimed my anger back at the real perpetrator

"For your information, nobody controls me, boyfriend, or not."

"He is." Lynch pointed toward the goon currently putting bruises on my arm.

"He's a square-shaped, ugly creep who beats his girlfriend."

"Who told you that?" Dirtbag said.

"Nobody, it's obvious that you're an ugly creep, although that is pretty disrespectful to creeps."

He yanked my arm so hard I collided with his huge body, setting off another string of visions. Out of the corner of my eye, I saw Logan step toward me.

"Did you talk to Greta?" Dirtbag asked.

"Who's Greta?"

He pointed at Logan with his free hand. "Or did he tell you?"

"He didn't know until now," I told him.

"Then who told you that lie?"

"Nobody cares," Lynch said. "Forget what she said, and let's get on with what we need to do."

I shrugged. "You might care that he's stealing from you."

"Montgomery's making up lies."

I was getting really tired of this ridiculous back and forth. I pulled at Square's grip on my arm. "Let go of me, you big ugly nuisance."

Release her," Lynch said. "It's not like she can get away from us."

"I wouldn't bet on that if I were you."

Lynch threw what was left of his cigarette on the

ground and stomped, "Enough of this. What are you doing in the woods hanging around a private business area?"

"Okay, you got me. I don't trust him," I pointed at Logan, "So when I saw his car, I decided to come this way and see if he was with another woman."

"So she *is* your girlfriend."

"I was until he dumped me. I'm just trying to figure out who she is." I looked Lynch right in the eye. "So I can make her regret what she's done."

He laughed so hard I thought he might fall to the ground. "Release her"

"But the lies—"

"She doesn't know anything. She's just trying to get under your skin and doing it very well."

"But—"

"I said, let her go!"

"Yes, sir." He released my arm, and without his hold, I almost landed on my derrière.

Suddenly I was being held up on the other side. "Are you okay?"

The lack of visions, coupled with the lack of pain, had me a bit lightheaded. "I just need a minute."

"I'm going to walk her to her car."

Lynch chuckled. "Take care of your little girlfriend."

Logan literally growled deep in his throat. "You don't have to be involved with someone to care that they're all right."

"Whatever. Just go so we can get back to work at some point."

Logan wrapped his arm around my waist and all but lifted me off the ground in his hurry to get away from there. I did my best to keep up with him, glad to be away. I let him use his strength to hold me up and keep me from tripping and landing on my face.

He stopped about halfway and guided me deeper into a copse of maple trees. "What were you thinking coming out here?"

"I was trying to sort things out. I'm sorry."

He tipped my chin up, and his gaze seemed to reach into my being. "Stay away, Dia. I don't want you to get hurt."

"I don't understand."

He pulled me into his arms. "I know you don't, and you have no real reason to trust me. I'm involved in a mess and the last thing I want is for you to get sucked in."

He looked back, then began edging me toward the trail. "Go to Terri's and stay there. I'll see you as soon as I can."

Soon we were at my car. He gave me a soft kiss, then headed back. As I started, I caught a glimpse of Logan watching. Likely making sure I was okay.

Damn, this was confusing.

Chapter 12

"Clear your mind and picture the person you want to connect with."

The words were calm, soothing, optimistic. My mind was crowded, confused, and worried. I tried. I kept shoving back distracting thoughts like I'd been told, but it was a losing fight.

"I'm sorry, Aunt Octavia. I just can't seem to focus."

We were in a gorgeous small clearing not far into the forest but hidden from easy view by large rocks and thick foliage. The better to shut out the outside world, my teacher had said.

"You have to trust yourself to focus. Trust is also key for making use of your intuition."

I looked down for a moment so Aunt Octavia wouldn't see the tears straining to come from my eyes. "'Myself' is the problem."

"Your heart and your mind are pulling in different directions. You have to reconcile them or choose which to follow."

I groaned. "There is no way to reconcile up and down, left and right, truth or fiction."

"What does your gift tell you?"

It was hard to tell her. "That Logan is involved in a plot that would hurt the Bigfoot tribe."

She nodded as if she already knew. Maybe she did.

"And your heart?"

I closed my eyes for a moment before I could say what I felt. "I can't believe the man I know could do something so awful."

"But you trust your gift more than your heart?"

The tears won, and I wiped them off my cheeks. "My visions have never been wrong."

"Have you ever misinterpreted a vision?"

The question caught me by surprise. "Not that I know of. They're usually pretty straightforward and clear."

"But this one was different?"

I shrugged. "I heard part of a conversation. "

"Which could be misinterpreted?"

"He says he can't explain right now, but that things are not what they seem." I dried my cheeks again. "He asked me not to give up on him."

"But you don't trust him."

My heart twisted. "I want to."

"Because you love him."

My attention jerked to her. "How did you know that?"

Aunt Octavia grinned. "It's easy to see love in a person's aura. Or in their face, for that matter."

"What should I do?"

"Only you can answer that question."

I thought about it for a bit. "I guess it wouldn't hurt to give him the benefit of the doubt." She nodded, and I continued. "If he's lying, It'll be obvious before long."

She hugged me. "It's important to trust your gift, but you have to trust your heart too. Especially since you and Logan are meant to be together."

"The soulmate thing."

She chuckled. "Don't be so reluctant to accept the notion. Soulmate is an age-old concept and very relevant to the world we live in today."

"Relevant how?"

Aunt Octavia grinned. "Folks today have forgotten about soulmates, and they don't have a clue how to know if they have one or if someone is their own. A lot of people don't even believe in love anymore. They mostly believe in violence and ugly and scary. People need to learn again that we have to take care of each other. It's the way we're hard-wired to live."

"So what does it mean, really, that Logan and I are soulmates? And what about Zook? Is there a reason we got a goat to deal with?"

"The two of you are soulmates, so you must learn to trust and care for each other. Each of you brings something different to the relationship making the two of you stronger than apart." She smiled. "The goat 'deal', as you call it, is simple. The two of you were given a creature to care for because without Zook, you wouldn't stay together long enough to figure out you belong together. I believe after a while, you'll discover you prefer having the little fuzzy creature around."

I gave her my skeptical look, and she chuckled. "Don't worry about that right now. The important thing is to figure out if you trust Logan and decide to give the relationship a shot. Got it?"

"I think so."

"Good, because you're needed at home."

****

When I pulled in the driveway, the scene that greeted me was one of utter chaos. Zook ran back and forth up and down the fence, making loud goat noises.

Terri and Hunter stood and stared at the furry troublemaker.

Terri rushed toward me. "I'm so glad you're back! Zook's upset, and we have no idea why."

"He's driving us bonkers," Hunter said.

I headed for the goat, who immediately came toward me.

"It's horrible." Zook was shaking.

"What's horrible?"

"The stench in that crazy woman's flower bed,"

"You said before there was a bad smell in there. Is this the same thing?"

"This ain't no regular little smelly, lady. What I got was a snoot full of nasty."

"Can you clarify a little? Nasty how?"

Zook's eyes seemed to go wild for a minute, rolling around like a kid was playing with them. "It was horrible. Horrible."

"Okay, horrible. But what kind of horrible? Seriously stinky? Something gross? Something that doesn't belong in the flowerbed?"

"Definitely doesn't belong in those delicious flowers."

I squatted so I'd be more at his level. "Just tell me, Zook, what did you smell?"

"Human."

I didn't know goats could whisper, but he did.

"What are you saying? Human how?"

"Human remains. Bones and such."

I was beginning to understand what had upset him. In fact, I was getting upset myself—and a little nauseated too. "Are you sure?"

"Yes, I'm sure." He trotted toward the house where

he found a big clump of grass and settled down to eat it.

"Wanna tell me what's wrong?" Terri put a hand on my shoulder. "You suddenly lost all the color in your face."

"Zook says there are human remains in that flower bed."

"I need to call my dad."

I nodded. "Creepy."

"Very." She squeezed my shoulder then headed toward the house.

I sat on the front steps, plopped my elbows onto my knees, then dropped my head into my hands. I came to Ugly Creek for some quiet time with my friend so that I could get past my crazy family. Instead, my life was just more complicated and crazy.

Then my phone let me know I had a text—and another layer of complication.

Chapter 13

The text was ambiguous.

—Meet me at the office. I have a surprise for you. Come on in, nobody's here.—

I rushed up the steps to the porch and yelled, "Gotta go, be back soon!" Then I bounced back down and jumped into my car. I quickly texted that I was on my way, then headed out.

As I drove, my mind struggled to figure out what he could possibly be up to. I reached for my phone, then thought better of it. Logan had texted for a reason, and I wasn't about to beg him for details. Sighing, I told myself I was a big girl, and I could survive without knowing what was happening for just a little while.

It felt like hours but was likely just a few short minutes as I drove through Ugly Creek and turned the corner toward New Century Research and Development. This late in the day, it wasn't a surprise there weren't any cars in the parking lot. Except one. A bright yellow convertible. Logan!

I parked next to him, grabbed my cell, and rushed toward the building. The door was probably locked. What would I do if it was? I supposed I'd have to go around the building looking for a way inside. He'd told me to come in; there had to be one.

There were four doors across the back entrance. Sure enough, the first one was locked, as was the second one. The third door opened easily, and I rushed headlong into whatever awaited.

The deserted building was so quiet the sound of my shoes clicking on the tile sounded like a warning. Maybe it was. I wanted to yell for Logan, but for some reason I couldn't explain, I didn't. Most of the doors were locked, and the unlocked ones led to dark, empty rooms that offered no indication that anybody was there. I felt silly for not calling out for Logan, but then, why hadn't he met me at the door? I had a bad feeling something wasn't quite right.

I heard footsteps and turned to greet Logan. Instead, Dirtbag grabbed me and picked me off the floor and threw me over his shoulder. I screamed, but the man holding me only laughed. Between his laugh and his huge, tattooed arms, I would have been freaked out enough, But added to that were the visions of his past treatment of women. He loved to hit, shove, and force them, and the pictures I saw were sickening.

Another man, this one unfamiliar, joined us. Dirtbag put my feet on the floor, and each of them took one of my arms. I pulled against them, but they didn't even seem to notice. I went limp, and they just kept going, dragging me along with them. I tried to get back to my feet, but they didn't stop. I yelled; I pulled; I tried to kick them. Nothing worked. They took me into a small room, and the door closed behind us.

"Well, hello. So glad you could join us."

Myles Lynch's voice made me gag.

"Look, Montgomery, your not-girlfriend is here."

I raised my head and saw Logan tied to a chair. His mouth was covered with tape, and bruises darkened his face. Tears sprang to my eyes. What the hell was going on? I struggled to my feet.

"How very nice of you to come." Lynch ran his hand over my hair, and I tried to kick at him. Unfortunately, he was out of range, and Dirtbag was tying my hands behind me.

Taking the one last opportunity before they managed to get me all trussed up, I pulled away from the goon. Before he could grab me again, I pivoted and decked Lynch. Blood spurted from his nose, and I swerved to nail Dirtbag, but he had his fist back.

"Telegraph much?"

I ducked the blow and threw my shoulder as hard as I could into Dirtbag's middle. He went down, and I fell on top of him. I immediately scrambled to my feet and took off toward the door.

I must have caught them by surprise because I got a few feet down the hall before the man I didn't recognize grabbed me and threw me to the floor. He tied my hands behind me, then jerked me to my feet and dragged me back to the little room. This time the door was locked behind us.

Lynch stood beside the chair where Logan was tied. I smirked a little when I looked his way. He leaned a little forward, one hand holding a handkerchief against his nose.

"I got you pretty good, huh?"

"Don't try it again." He slid his free hand from behind Logan to reveal some sort of hunting knife with a brown handle and a big blade. He pressed the knife against Logan's throat until blood formed on Logan's skin.

"No!"

Lynch smiled. "What I do depends on you."

"Fine, I'll behave." At least for now.

Lynch moved the knife. "Smart girl."

"Woman."

Lynch chuckled. He jerked the tape off Logan's mouth.

"Are you all right, Dia?" Logan caught my gaze, and anguish in his eyes tore at my heart.

"I'm okay," I told him. "Worried about you, though."

He snorted. "I'm great."

"Good," Lynch said. "Then you're ready to tell me who you're working for."

"I've told you repeatedly. I work for the same company you do."

Lynch stepped around in front of the chair and slapped Logan across the face so hard the sound made my ears ring. "Who are you really working for? Who are you spying for? "

Lynch walked toward me, and I caught a glimpse of the extreme redness on the side of Logan's face. He blinked rapidly, and I realized he was fighting back the tears from the slap.

Lynch stepped in front of me. "Do you know what your boyfriend is really doing?"

"Sure, he's a dancer for Ballet Russe."

"You think you're funny, don't you?"

"I'm funnier than you, but that's not saying much."

He paced and I could see Logan again. He gave me a smile that made me very proud.

"Maybe she can help convince you to tell me what I want to know."

I narrowed my eyes and gave him the hardest look I could dredge up. "I won't help you."

"I didn't say it would be voluntary." He held up the knife from earlier and pressed the blade against my arm. He increased the pressure and slowly drew it from one side to the other. Blood seeped out, ran over my arm, and dripped onto the floor. I ground my teeth to keep from crying out. He held my arm still with his other hand, and I saw visions that made me gag.

"Well, Montgomery, are you ready to start talking now?"

"That tickled," I said.

Lynch slapped me across the face. I blinked back tears and looked into the man's eyes. "That's all you have? What are you, a little girl?"

"Don't, Dia. He's a bad man."

Lynch spun to look at Logan. "You know nothing about me."

"Actually, I know a lot about you. Things like your wife died under strange circumstances, and you are still the number one suspect."

Lynch's face turned almost as red as Logan's after he'd been slapped. "How do you know that?."

Logan shrugged. "It's amazing what's on the Internet."

"That's not online." He turned away for a moment. "It's not true."

"Oh, yes it is."

"You like your females very young. You sick SOB."

He jerked around to glare at me, his face almost purple by now. "Talking, talking, talking, and still not telling me what I want to know."

"Why do you care if I'm working for someone else?" Logan asked.

"Because I like to keep our discoveries away from competitors."

My last nerve snapped, and before I could hold it back, my temper flared. "Like what you're planning to do to Bigfoot?"

Lynch's eyes went wide and his face purpled. But he immediately turned his attention back to Logan. "You told her, you idiot! Are you trying to get us in trouble with the government?"

"No, just you. I'm a spy for the FBI."

I focused my gaze on Logan, wondering if continuing to antagonize his boss up was really a good idea.

Lynch laughed. "That's a good one." He held up his knife. Now let's see how your girlfriend looks after some facial surgery."

The door literally exploded, and suddenly the room was full of people with guns.

"FBI! Hands in the air!"

My mouth dropped open. He was telling the truth.

The next few minutes were a whirl. Lynch and his two goons arrested. Somebody cut me loose from the chair. I was shaky, but it felt good to be on my feet. Then I was pulled into a familiar pair of strong arms.

"Are you all right, sweetheart?"

I touched Logan's face. "Yes, are you?"

"I'm fine as long as you are."

One of the agents pressed some gauze against my arm.

"I'll do that," he told the woman, and took over holding it against my cut.

All at once, tears filled my eyes. "I was so afraid they were going to hurt you."

"I was terrified for you." He pulled me firmly against him. "Why in the world were you even here?"

"You texted me."

"I what?"

"You texted me." The truth hit hard. I handed him my phone, then let my forehead fall against his firm chest. "I was tricked."

He held me protectively against him. "I'm just glad you're not hurt any worse than you are. I couldn't stand it if anything happened to you. I love you, Dia. I love you so much it scares me sometimes."

"I love you too," I said.

Logan leaned in to touch his lips to mine, and for a moment, it was just the two of us.

"Okay, we need statements from you two. Both of you also need to be checked to make sure you're okay. Come with me," the agent said and herded us outside toward a waiting ambulance.

A woman in black pants and a paramedic jacket was already gloved, and it only took a moment to exchange the gauze on my cut for cleaning and a bandage. The wound hurt but I didn't care. We'd survived without serious injury. A little pain only proved I was alive. She made us both sit, gave me a quick look over, took my blood pressure and pulse, then repeated the procedure with Logan.

A few minutes later, we were pronounced healthy enough to be interrogated. The agent who had walked us out came over, I assumed, to interview us.

"Dia, this is Special Agent Max Killian." Logan said, "He's the man in charge of keeping Ugly Creek safe. I was working with him to put Lynch away without compromising any of the town's specialness."

"Nice to meet you," I said. "I'll do whatever I can to help.

"I'm thrilled to hear that. But your statements can wait. Something is going on at your friend's house," he said.

"Terri's house?"

"Well, technically her aunt's house, but yeah." Killian hurried toward the parking lot, and its assortment of vehicles.

"What in the world could be going on at Hunter and Terri's house?" Logan asked as we rushed toward our cars.

"Meet you there," I said. Logan didn't look too happy, but he nodded.

I shrugged. After everything that had happened, I thought I could believe almost anything.

Still, I couldn't have imagined the sight when I turned onto Terri's road. A sheriff's car was parked on the road in front of the house, along with two other cars, one black, one dark blue. I recognized both of them from the parking lot at New Century Research and Development.

Sheriff's deputy Ken Bennett stood away from everybody, back turned, a cell phone to his ear.

Shay and Ace were there, and Stephie and Jake. Of course, Terri and Hunter were there. I pulled into the driveway. Hunter held Zook by a red rope around his neck, and everybody else milled around near them.

I headed for Terri, who was already coming toward me. "What the crap is going on?"

"We reported the smell of decomposition Zook told us about."

"But humans can't smell it."

"Hunter spoke to Ken, the deputy, who's lived here his whole life." He didn't ask too many questions, but he did ask if we had any ideas about how to verify our *suspicions.*'"

"What did you tell him?"

"That I had an idea." She shrugged. "So I called my dad, and I told him what Zook said. So now he's checking with his FBI connections."

There was something off about that sentence. "Wait, did you tell your dad a goat told me he smelled human remains?"

Terri snorted. "Dad's a wolf-collie hybrid shapeshifter. I think he'll be all right."

"I remember now; you said he'd smelled something before."

She nodded. "Human decomposition. But Miz C kept him from getting close enough to verify that."

"So, we don't know for sure what's over there?"

"Well, I trust Dad's nose, but that gets us nowhere as far as the rest of the legal system is concerned."

"Would it help if I found out something? It wouldn't be admissible in court, but then knowledge is power, after all."

Terri shrugged. "Your call, girlfriend. You're the one who has to deal with the repercussions."

I looked toward the woman standing near her flowerbed. I didn't know her, but everything I'd seen or heard about her had me believing she was a strong, mean woman.

"Let's do this thing." I headed toward the white picket fence that separated the yards. The fence wasn't very high, so I stepped over it.

"Miz Carlisle," I called out. "Are you all right?"

"Of course I am." I headed bravely toward her, and as she got closer, I saw she was trembling.

"I don't know what y'all got up over there, but I'm not stupid. I know it's got something to do with me."

"Don't worry about that. You know crazy stuff happens all the time in this town."

Her eyes narrowed, but she nodded. "That's true."

"It's probably all a big misunderstanding."

She was close enough I could put my hand on her arm. My head filled with dark images of a couple.

"You're worthless!" a younger version of Miz Carlisle yelled.

"Would ya lay off me, woman?"

"I want nice things. I want to go on vacation to new places. I want to—"

"You want me to be a rich man, and you knew when you married me that I wasn't!"

"Well, I thought you'd at least get out there and try to give me what I want."

"I've got news for you, Edith. I'm not gonna kill myself just so you can fit in with your snobby friends."

"You are a horrible man."'

"Well, you ain't no great prize yourself."

"Why did I marry the likes of you?"

"Because nobody else would have your fat ass." He sat in a big recliner and flipped on the TV.

She moved behind him, raised her arms, and brought a hammer down hard.

Blood squirted up and out like a gory ocean wave covering both of them.

He rolled out of the chair and onto the floor, blood still pouring from his head.

"So long, horrible man." Then she let out a long,

shrill laugh.

I gasped and looked into the face of a murderer. "You killed him!"

"I don't know what you're talking about?" Mrs. Carlisle backed away from me, her face pasty and her eyes wide.

Strong arms wrapped around me and gently pulled me back against a big warm body.

"Logan."

"I've got you, sweetheart." He turned me away from the crazy woman, and we beat a hasty retreat back to the other yard.

"She killed her husband," I whispered.

"Poor guy." Logan gave me a little squeeze. "You need to sit."

I perched on the porch step. The horrible vision wouldn't let up. All I could do was wait.

A black sedan pulled up, and Max Killian got out. He opened the passenger door for a big dog. I glanced toward Carlisle. Her eyes widened, and she rushed to scoop up her cat, who'd been watching the proceedings from a few feet away.

"I need to talk to Max," I said.

"Okay." Logan held my hand as we headed toward the FBI agent.

Terri hurried over. Like her alter ego, this dog had collie genes, but unlike her, he was larger and wilder looking. To me, he seemed very wolf-like. Was this her dad? Freaky.

I gave Max a quick run-down of what I'd seen when I touched Carlisle. "Too bad that won't get us a warrant to search her property," he said. "But at least we know we're barking up the right tree."

The dog whimpered a bit.

Likely because he wasn't the current center of attention, Zook started making annoyingly loud sounds. The newcomer dog gave the goat a sharp bark, then bumped Terri's leg.

"Dia and Logan's goat. He talks to them."

The wolf-dog looked at her and gave a sharp little bark.

"Yes," she said. "He smelled something, and that's why I called you."

"It was good to hear from your dad, Terri. I've always enjoyed working with him. I'll be looking forward to working with him again."

Max and the dog strolled over toward the fence. We followed behind them at a casual pace.

"What is that creature?" Miz Carlisle called from several feet away.

Max laughed. "Don't worry about Boomer here. He's an old friend of mine. We used to work together."

"You worked with a dog?" Disdain dripped from her words.

"Yes, I did. And I enjoyed every minute of it."

"I don't believe you. What did he do, bite the bad guys?"

"No. Boomer here is a cadaver dog."

"A what?"

"A cadaver dog. They help recover bodies from disaster sites and find graves."

I wouldn't have thought it possible, but Carlisle's face paled further.

"That sounds like a disgusting line of work."

Max shrugged. "It can be pretty rough at times, but it's an important job that allows families to get closure and the dead to be buried properly."

"Still sounds horrid to me." She sniffed.

Max shrugged. "To each his own."

Boomer slowly edged toward the flower bed.

Ms. C saw the movement and hurried toward him. She held her cat close to one side with one hand and made huge shooing motions with the other hand. Boomer backed away.

"Keep that smelly thing out of my flowers."

"Yes, ma'am." He motioned with his chin, and we all trotted back toward the house.

"Anything?" Ken asked.

Max shook his head. "She's won't let us near her flowers without a warrant."

Ken sighed. "Not an easy thing to get on the word of a magical goat and a shapeshifting dog."

"Don't forget the psychic newcomer," Max said.

Ken looked at me. "You?"

I nodded. "When I touch people, I get visions of their lives."

He groaned. "Peachy."

"I know it's not any help with warrants and courts, but I saw what happened. Knowing details might come in handy."

That caught his interest. "You have a point there. Why don't you tell us what you saw, and I'll go from there."

We retired to the porch steps to talk, and I told him all about my visions and and what I'd seen when I touched Miz Carlisle. Then he and Ken had a conference, and Ken took off.

I went in search of Logan, which didn't take long since he waited nearby. He pulled me in close and kissed me until my legs wouldn't hold my body up Being a gentleman, he tucked me against his warm, strong body so that I wouldn't fall.

"As soon as the show's over, I'd like to go to my place and have a long, intimate conversation."

"Intimate, huh?"

"Oh yeah."

Terri and Hunter, with the assistance of Shay and Ace, made sandwiches for everybody. So we sat on the porch and ate cold cuts on whole wheat sandwiches while we waited.

Across the fence, Miz Carlisle paced, picked up, and put down her cat so much that he finally ran away. She kept calling him and seemed to be genuinely worried, but I didn't have the heart to turn him in for hiding under a bush with Terri's cat.

It was getting dark when Ken returned, handed a sheet of paper to Max, and the two of them walked away from everybody. Boomer joined them, lying on the ground and pretending not to understand anything.

About five minutes later, the fireworks began.

Chapter 14

Logan and I sat on the front steps and looked on as the drama unfolded.

"You can't just walk in here like you own the place!"

Ken held up the paper. "Ma'am, this is a warrant, signed by a judge, giving us permission to search your property."

"That can't be right. I'm calling my lawyer!"

"Go right ahead. Meanwhile, Agent Killian and I will be looking around."

Max, with Boomer on a leash, began a slow round of her front yard, moving closer and closer to the flower bed.

"Oh no. You can't have that stinky, flea-growing monster in here."

"Actually, we can," Ken told her. "The search warrant states that we may use trained dogs to assist us."

Carlisle's eyes widened. "You can't do this. This is my home! You're trespassing." She pointed toward the road. "Go!"

"You're welcome to call your lawyer, but we have a legal search warrant, and we're going to search."

"I'm calling my son and my lawyer. They'll make you leave."

"Go right ahead, ma'am."

While Ken and Miz C argued, Max and Boomer reached the edge of her flower bed. Ken stayed near her front porch, apparently watching for any signs of trouble. A few minutes later, he was joined by two other deputies. They talked for a few minutes, then separated and took up positions on each side of the yard, A few minutes later, my cell buzzed. I groaned as I took the call.

"What did I do now?"

"You were right." The voice was faint, and I heard a sniffle.

"Finley, what's wrong?"

"I wanted to talk to him. I just wanted to talk." She paused for a minute, and the pain coming through the line was almost palpable.

"I went to his apartment." She swallowed. "Scott and Laura were in the living room. On the couch."

For a moment, all I heard was my sister crying.

"Are you okay, sis?"

"You were right like you always are. I just really wanted to believe he was a good guy."

"Oh, Finley. I'm so sorry." I wiped the tears from my eyes. "Is there anything I can do?"

"Not really. I just wanted to let you know you were right. I'm sorry I treated you so awful. I love you, Diara."

"I love you too, little sis."

We hung up, and I returned to the steps by Logan.

"Everything all right?" he asked.

"Finley caught her fiancé and her best friend together."

"So you were right."

"Yeah, but I wish I'd been wrong."

"I know." He pulled me into his arms, and I snuggled against him.

****

Within a few minutes, Boomer indicated he'd found something. They tried to explain to Miz Carslie that there was nothing she could do. Her son arrived, and he too tried to explain that the police and FBI had the legal right to search.

She was still livid when the lawyer handed his card to the son and left. Mr. Carlisle, the son, tried to calm her down, but she continued to march back and forth, yelling it was her yard, and nobody had the right to be there. He finally sat on the edge of his mother's porch and watched her. The only time he moved was if she got too close to the police officers. Then he led her away and stood speaking quietly to her until she calmed down.

More FBI arrived along with the coroner. They cordoned off the flower bed, and began sectioning the area into a grid. As the sun lowered, the temperature dropped. A gust of cool late afternoon spring air sent shivers through my body, and Logan wrapped his jacket around my shoulders.

"Thank you," I whispered.

He took my hand in his, and with his other, traced the wound on my upper arm. "I should have been more careful."

"Hey, I was the one who kept sticking my nose in."

'True," he said.

I raised an eyebrow.

He shifted so that he was closer. "I should have taken better care of you."

"Hey," I looked deep into his dark eyes, and my

heart stuttered. "I'm a grown woman. I don't need anybody to take care of me."

"You do when you're tricked into a trap by your boyfriend's boss. I should have told you to stay away from me."

I reached up to touch his cheek. "There's nothing you could have said that would have kept me away from you. I was worried."

"That I was seeing somebody else?"

"No, not really. I just knew something wasn't right."

He laughed. "I think you do read me somehow. If the situation were reversed, I would have been looking for a guy to pound into the dirt."

"Jealous?"

"Hell, yeah."

"Okay, I was a little jealous," I told him. "But I was also worried about you."

Logan shook his head. "You shouldn't have been. I'm the one who signed up for the spying thing. You weren't working with all the information you needed to make good choices. For instance, I knew Max was listening and that he'd rescue me, but you didn't."

Anger lashed out like a bolt of lightning. "He was listening, but he let you get tortured?"

Logan shrugged. "I was okay."

"No, you weren't."

"He wanted to wait until Lynch had admitted to not caring about the Bigfoot tribe."

"No matter the cost to you?"

He pulled me against his firm chest. "Honey, I knew the risks when I agreed to take Lynch down. He's a horrible man who needs to spend the rest of his life behind bars."

I looked up at him, even knowing he'd see my tears. "You could have died!"

He shook his head. "I trust Max."

"I don't."

"I know." He brushed a tear off my cheek. "You were the one I was worried about. We'd worked hard for months to set Lynch up. I knew Max wouldn't deliberately put you in harm's way, but he might let things go too far without realizing the danger you were in." He abruptly looked down and swiped across his eyes with the back of his hand.

"Logan?" I touched a finger to the tear running down his cheek.

"I couldn't stand it if you'd been hurt." He swallowed. "And it would have been my fault."

I pulled him close, and he buried his face in my hair.

"I love you," he whispered. "And I want you in my life."

Everything abruptly fell into place. All the little jagged pieces of my crazy life slipped into a nice, neat, logical pattern.

"I love you too," I told him. "And I want you in my life too."

Logan pulled back just enough to meet my gaze. He smiled, and his eyes lit up with happiness. He leaned closer slowly, inch by maddening inch, until his lips were about to touch mine.

"There's a body in here."

We froze as we shared a moment of frustration before both of us turned to see police swarming the area around the flower bed. Miz C screamed at the top of her lungs about her rights and how they were being violated.

I glanced toward the bushes at the side of Terri's house where the cats stared at the ruckus. Good, at least the crazy woman's cat was safe.

"Told ya so!"

I was startled enough that I squealed. Zook, damn it, let out a sound that was half-bleet, half-laugh. I gave him my best glare, but he only made the sound again.

"Hey, Zook," Logan squatted in front of the goat. "Why don't you stay here tonight? You'll be sure not to miss anything, and it'd give Dia and me a little alone time."

"Are you kidding? And miss the two of you finally figuring out that you really are soulmates? Not a chance."

"You're a mean little goat," I told him.

"Naw, just doing my job."

Logan looked up at me. "I tried."

"Yes, you did."

He took me into his arms again. Across the fence, Terri's aunt's neighbor was being taken in for questioning regarding the death of whoever was in her flower bed.

"He deserved it!" she yelled. "That no good husband of mine deserved killing. I should have done a lot sooner.

She was handcuffed, read her rights and put in the back of Ken's police cruiser. As he pulled out, she was still yelling about how horrible the man was.

Miz C's son stood to one side. I sucked in air as the reality hit me. His mother had murdered his father in cold blood. His pain was palpable to me, even this far away. Poor guy, he was going to have a rough time of it.

My attention was caught by Terri rushing toward me. She slid to a stop just before crashing and knocking both of us to the ground.

"I knew she was nuts," Terri announced. "But I had no idea she was murderer nuts."

"Nuts or evil?" Logan asked.

"Looks pretty nuts to me," Terri said.

"She lived with him, with what she'd done," I said. "All those years, he was right there, where she'd buried him. In her flowers, where she worked every single day to protect her secret. She had to be haunted."

"By his ghost?" Terri's eyes had widened.

"Maybe," I said. "Or just by the knowledge of what she'd done."

"Assuming she isn't a psychopath."

I shivered at the thought, and Logan gently massaged my shoulder. "That feels wonderful," I said.

Terri grinned. "Maybe I should leave you two alone."

"Actually, we'll leave you alone if you would be so kind as to watch after our furry, big-mouthed pain."

"I'd be happy to." She scratched behind Zook's ears.

He looked like he would melt.

"You can't do this," the goat said.

Logan raised an eyebrow. "We're going to a hotel somewhere that isn't here, and you can't come."

Zook leaned into Terri's hand. "I guess I have to concede this time."

"Good, because I have something to talk to Dia about and a question to ask her."

Terri let out a little squeal. "I get to be your maid of honor."

"Down, girl," I said. "You're jumping about three steps in a direction we aren't even sure we're going in."

"Oh, get real, girlfriend. Your man is about to pr—"

"Stuff it, Quinn!" Logan placed his palms on both sides of Terri's face. "You take care of Zook, and let us take care of our lives."

"Okay." She led Zook away with a hand in the fur on his neck.

****

We threw together a few things and headed out of town. To my surprise, Logan pulled the car over at the spot where he'd almost run me off the road. "This is where we met."

I looked into his beautiful eyes. "Where you almost ran me over."

He gently touched my face. "I'd never hurt you."

Maybe I was delusional, but I believed this enigmatic, sweet, and amazing "bad boy."

"I know."

"Do you?"

"I do."

He grinned. "Remember those words."

My breath caught as he pulled a small box from a pocket. He opened it to reveal a simple, elegant ring. It was so beautiful it took my breath away.

"You like it?"

"I love it. But it's not your usual showy style."

"You taught me something."

"What's that?"

"That money is not nearly as important as the

people you love, and I love you."

"I love you too."

He slid the ring on my left hand and held it gently. "Will you marry me, Dia Grey?"

Tears ran from my eyes, and I wiped at them. "I'd be honored."

He kissed me long and gently. Then he put his yellow car in gear and we headed off for a few days of sheer bliss.

A word about the author...

Cheryel Hutton talks to a dragon named Quill, who is actually a legendary Muse who chooses to live in the form of a dragon.

She talks to Cheryel too, and together they write stories of witches, werewolves, bigfoot creatures, fairies, and vampires. Some of the stories are light and funny, and some are dark and scary. They also write stories of evil humans—and those are the scariest stories of all.

After her husband passed away, Cheryel's adult daughters wanted her to live closer to them. So she moved near Nashville, Tennessee where she talks with her dragon, enjoys spending time with her grandchildren, and enjoys the inspiring beauty of the South.

****

http://www.cheryelhutton.com

****

If you enjoyed this story, leaving a review at your favorite book retailer or reader website would be much appreciated. Thank you!